The *he*

Storm

Celtic Highland Maidens
Book 1

Michelle Deerwester-Dalrymple

The Maiden of the Storm

Copyright 2020 Michelle Deerwester-Dalrymple All rights reserved
ISBN: 9798683920296
Imprint: Independently published

Solstice prayer:
https://www.owlsdaughter.com/2010/06/blessings-of-litha-the-summer-soltstice/

Caim prayer:
https://www.waymarkers.net/blog/2017/09/14/rewilding-prayer-how-caim-invites-protection-for-all-of-creation

All rights reserved. In accordance with the U.S. Copyright Act of 1976, the scanning, uploading, distribution, or electronic sharing of any part of this book without the permission of the author constitutes unlawful piracy of the author's intellectual property. If you would like to use the material from this book, other than for review purposes, prior authorization from the author must be obtained. Copies of this text can be made for personal use only. No mass distribution of copies of this text is permitted.

This book is a work of fiction. Names, dates, places, and events are products of the author's imagination or used factiously. Any similarity or resemblance to any person living or dead, place, or event is purely coincidental.

The Maiden of the Storm

Table of Contents

Chapter One: We Should Keep Him	5
Chapter Two: Intriguing Beyond Measure	9
Chapter Three: Won't They Come for Him?	27
Chapter Four: Laws of the Land	45
Chapter Five: What Else Could a Man Want?	53
Chapter Six: Questionable Intentions	58
Chapter Seven: High Summer Festival	73
Chapter Eight: Morning After Realizations	85
Chapter Nine: Nothing to Regret	97
Chapter Ten: A Strategic Plan	108
Chapter Eleven: Liberation	122
Chapter Twelve: Betrayal and Punishment	133
Chapter Thirteen: Running for His Life	148
Chapter Fourteen: An Ironic Twist of Fate	153
Chapter Fifteen: A Surprise on the Ship	164
Chapter Sixteen: How to Take Advantage of a Bad Situation	171
Chapter Seventeen: Limited Options	179
Chapter Eighteen: Seaside Reunions	190
Chapter Nineteen: A Rag-Tag Band of Travelers	201
Chapter Twenty: A Fine Welcome Home	210
Chapter Twenty-One: What Happens When Love Wins	216
Excerpt from The Maiden of the Grove	223
A Note on History	227
A thank you to my readers –	229
About the Author	230
Also by the Author:	231

The Maiden of the Storm

Chapter One: We Should Keep Him

Northern Scotland, north of Antoine's Wall, Caledonii Tribe, 209 AD

RUMORS CIRCULATED of Roman Centauriae extending their patrols north beyond Antoine's wall, what they referred to disdainfully as *cnap-starra*. And her father's tribe watched from their secluded positions as those soldiers behaved in stupid, overly confident ways. If they wouldn't have risked giving away their positions, the painted men might have laughed at the ill-mannered soldiering of these weighted-down Romans.

Ru was chieftain of his tribe, a remote relative of the great King Gartnaith Blogh who himself managed to run the Roman fools from the Caledonii Highlands. 'Twas said the king laughed with zeal as the Latin devils, in their flaying and rusted

Roman armor, scrambled over the low stone wall. As though a minor *cnap-starra* could stop the mighty Caledonii warriors from striking fear into the heart of their Centauriae. Fools.

But speculation blossomed of rogue Roman soldiers venturing far north of the wall, a reckless endeavor if Ru's daughter, Riana, ever heard one. Warriors from her father's tribe and other nearby tribes traveled across the mountainous countryside, through the wide glen to meet them.

Thus far, the soldiers had remained close to the wall, fearing to leave the false security it provided. Ru's warriors had struck down one or two that meandered away from that security, wounding them, perchance fatally, with a well-aimed throw of a spear. The diminutive Roman soldiers, even clad in their hopeful leather and metal armor, were no match for the powerful throw of a Caledonii spear.

This most recent Roman soldier, however, appeared less resilient, less aggressive than his previous counterparts. Though clad in full Roman military garb, he wasn't paying attention to his surroundings — distracted as he was. The Centauriae had traversed the low mountains and lochs to their hidden land. And he was alone. Ru noted his lean-muscled build and made an abrupt decision.

"Dinna kill this lad," he whispered to Dunbraith, his military adviser and old friend. "We should keep him, enslave him. Melt his iron and armor into weapons. And use his knowledge against these pissants. Give them a bit of their own medicine."

Dunbraith's face, blue woad paint lines mixed with blood red, was fearsome and thoughtful. "Severus is defeated," his growling voice responded. "The Roman lines are scattered. 'Tis a safe assumption they will not even try to retrieve the lad."

A frightening smile crossed his face, one that Ru knew well. A cruel smile that didn't reach his eyes.

Ru nodded his agreement and waved his hand at his *Imannae*, a young Caledonii eager to prove his worth. The young man positioned himself just beyond the leaves of the scrub bush in which he hid, narrowed his eyes at his prey, and launched a strong-armed throw of his sharpened spear.

The *Imannae's* throw was perfect, catching the young Roman's upper arm in a sharp drive. The lad cried out and dropped to his knees in pain and shock. Ru and his warriors moved in as silent as nightfall.

***

The men who came upon Horatio as he recoiled on the seeping ground (*how did they live in so much wet?* he thought wildly) were large, painted monsters from his nightmares. He hadn't believed his older cohorts when they regaled the younger men with stories of fighting lore, describing the Highland men as blue and green giants.

Yet, here they were, these impossible creatures of haunted stories, and he was injured, outnumbered, and sending up his prayers to the gods. He immediately regretted his night of drinking with his fellow Legionnaires. His life in this world had certainly been short, and he was not prepared to see it end yet.

They made low grunting sounds, then grabbed him by the shoulder plates and dragged his limp form over the damp grass. Horatio wanted to fight back, but even the slightest wiggle inflamed his already pounding shoulder wound. He struggled to even move the arm, let alone fight with it.

The fact they were dragging him off perplexed him. Why didn't they just slay him where he fell? Surely, they weren't taking him elsewhere to kill him — that made little sense. Nor did it fit what he knew of their fierce hit-and-run tactics that had defeated the Roman Legions. Where were they taking him? And why didn't they have on any footwear?

After what seemed like hours, a palisade brightened by firelight glowed in the distance. The two mammoth men who appeared to be the leaders dragged him past a gate into an inner bailey. Dozens of round, thatched houses were scattered within this palisade. *Their homes?* he pondered in a bleary cloud. Though many were dark, their inhabitants asleep, Horatio assumed, two of the wider round houses were well lit, awaiting their arrival.

Horatio's arm throbbed, his body ached, and his brain pounded in a fevered panic. He couldn't begin to guess what they would do to him next.

Chapter Two: Intriguing Beyond Measure

RIANA WATCHED AS her father and his menacing adviser led the men to their door, throwing a dirt-encrusted form near her feet. She stood with her sister, Aila, watching her father with a measured expression. Life had calmed since the supposed peace treaty with the Romans, the lie that it was, yet here was her father bringing conflict right to their village gates. Riana bit the inside of her cheek and shared a knowing look with her sister. *Typical.*

Temperance was not their father's strong suit.

The evening's damp air combated the warmer air of the wheelhouse, and Riana gathered her woolen plaid *arasaid* more tightly around her shoulders. After her father's men deposited the dirty figure on the floor, they gave him curt bows and departed. Only Ru and Dunbraith remained.

"Take care of the man, will ye, Aila? Riana will help ye. Bandage up his arm. Make sure he has use of it. He will need it shortly to work in our clan."

"Work in our clan?" Riana asked, spinning to her father as he made his way to the door. "What do ye mean?"

Ru sighed at his daughter, hating how she always managed to second guess him. His oldest child, the eldest of six daughters, she most resembled her mother many years since dead. Her deep red hair, like blood on the earth, fell about her shoulders in wild pandemonium, untamed by circlet or headdress. She wore it loose, in the way of the Caledonii, long and curly.

Of a fair size and the tallest of her sisters, Riana exuded a sense of leadership and authority that burned from the green of her eyes. Her ferocious sense of responsibility was a gift from him, that Ru well knew. She could command any man of the tribe with a flick of her head. She reminded him of his own youth, an unfortunate trait in a daughter.

At least she wasn't always taking off with a bow at her back, unlike her younger sister. Who wanted to marry a willful warrior woman who also served as the hunter? What would be left for her husband to do?

Not that anyone had yet asked, Ru thought with a moue of grief. Most young men cowered in the shadows of the bear-like chieftain and his warriors, thus few dared to ask after the lass. Nor had men Ru encountered met his own lofty standards as potential suitors for any of his daughters.

And though he wore his tough exterior in the same manner that the Romans wore their armor, when it came to his daughters, he was pudding on the inside. And for his firstborn daughter of his tribe, Riana, he had the softest heart.

Until recently, when several of her actions threatened her safety and the security of the family and tribal village. Her delicate features and smooth, womanly skin belied a sharp tongue that questioned every decision he'd made as of late, and his temper reared its ugly face to Riana more often than he cared to admit.

So when she questioned him this night, in front of the injured Roman and his man at arms, 'twas the last straw. He bit the inside of his mouth to stop the roar of anger that erupted inside him, yet his words still held a tone as sharp as a dirk.

"Lass, the man needs to use the arm, as a one-armed slave is of no value to me," he growled at his daughter, putting her in her place.

Aila froze where she crouched by the downed man, her own hazel-green eyes wide with fright at the conflict between her sister and father. The mention of slavery could only make that conflict worse. Ru flicked his eyes from one sister to the other.

"Help Aila heal the man so he can live."

The giant of a chieftain gave his defiant daughter a final glare and exited the roundhouse into the cloak of night.

Riana remained rooted where she stood, mouth agape and shamed at being chastised like a bairn. Her face burned as red as the fire in the center hearth. She daren't look at her younger sister out of fear of losing the tears that welled up in her eyes and threatened to fall.

"Riana," Aila called to her, breaking the uncomfortable silence. "Help me with the man, aye?"

Grateful for the distraction, Riana wiped at her eyes with her *arasaid* draped around her shoulders and moved to her sister's side. Scarcely shorter than Riana, Aila's interests lay far from leadership and confrontations with her father — rather she saw herself as the healer for the camp, hoping one day to continue her training under a crone-healer to learn everything she could.

As part of her commitment to healing, Aila believed she needed to remain untouched. To accomplish this, she wrapped any skin exposed, from her low-belted *léine* and plaid *arasaid* she tucked into the belt, in strips of flax linen. Only her fingertips showed, dainty stubs tinged green by herbs.

Unlike Riana, Aila also wore a flower-bedecked headdress that covered her neck and much of her hair, with only vermilion curls escaping around her pale face that she painted with thin stripes of blue woad. If she weren't a full healer in her own mind, she surely presented herself as an accomplished one in her outward appearance.

Tonight, they needed to rely on whatever healing skills Aila did have to treat the man. Riana lifted the man's strange tunic, noting the stain of blood. 'Twasn't the wound itself that worried either Aila or Riana, 'twas if pus set into the wound. Any man could recover from a strike to the shoulder — the Caledonii oft continued fighting with several similar wounds from head to toe. Recovering from the curse of heated pus, however . . .

Riana caught Aila's matching verdant gaze as she squatted next to the man's head. They both knew the horrific ending to that curse.

"Have ye the herbs to treat the lad?" Riana asked.

Aila snorted. "Nay a lad, a full man just with lean muscle. His chest is wholly formed, which means he is well-fed, and we can hope he is hale to boot. 'Tis quite possible since he is a soldier. If he be that, then the herbs I have should work. Praise Airmid."

"Praise Airmid," Riana echoed. Calling on the Goddess of Healing may not help, but 'twouldn't hurt, and they needed every bit of assistance they could get to heal this wounded Roman. And appease their chieftain father.

"Put him on my pallet," Riana directed, clasping him as gently as she could under his injured arm.

The Maiden of the Storm

Aila grabbed his other arm, and they dragged him to her padded tartan pallet, flipping the furs to the side so he didn't bleed all over them.

Riana flicked her privacy curtain wide open. Then, turning to the fire at the center of the roundhouse, she fed it a handful of peat, its flames providing a dancing light by which Aila could treat her poor patient.

And truly, 'twas what Riana thought of the Roman. Ripped from his Legion, assaulted and left bleeding on the floor, and now needing the surgical aid of a young, untested woman. Poor man indeed.

Though his body pained him, the man had remained silent, unmoving, which worried Riana. What if the man didn't wake? Riana moved to toe him in the ribs when Aila spoke.

"Help me remove his tunic, so I can properly treat his arm."

The Roman was limp as they tugged and yanked before finally pulling the stained garment from the man. Riana gave it a sniff and in a quick decision tossed it into the fire. He would be given fresh clothes reflecting his enslaved status once he recovered.

If he recovered.

"Do ye have the skills for this Aila? His wound seems significant."

Aila's studious face didn't shift but remained intent on the now-seeping wound. Small beads of sweat glittered across her forehead. She sniffed in disgust at Riana's implication of any lack in her skills.

"'Tis no less than Eian's wound these months past," Aila answered in a low, flat tone.

She stuck her finger inside the open wound to make sure none of the spear remained. The Roman's reaction was sharp and immediate.

The Maiden of the Storm

His back arched as he inhaled a screech. He thrashed about, trying to throw the women off. Riana pressed her weight on his torso, and the man stilled, gasping loudly.

"Weel, we ken he's no' dead," Riana stated.

Aila retrieved a bowl of hot water from the pot above the hearth. Her stark gaze caught Riana's. "Hold him again. He will no' like this."

She poured the scalding water into the wound. This time the man screamed before passing out completely.

Riana placed her hand on his forehead, whispering calm cooing sounds. Aila scrubbed the wound briskly, then added several grains and crumbled dried leaves, mostly figwort, into the water left in the *quaich* goblet. She mixed that into a paste that stunk up the entire roundhouse.

Crinkling her nose in distaste, Riana ran her hand over the odd, short hair of the Roman as though he were a child. He stayed still enough at her efforts, allowing Aila to apply a thick layer of paste into and over the wound. She then wrapped his arm with strips of flaxen linen, protecting it while it healed.

"'Tis in Airmid's hands now," Aila said. "We will ken in a day or so if feverish pus sets in. If it does, his woes regarding enslavement are over, as he'll die soon. But he seems a strapping man. Mayhap he is strong enough to heal well."

"Ye forgot the third possibility. If the arm is diseased, he may lose the arm, and father shall turn him out on his own devices, where he'll surely perish. Poor lad. 'Twould appear all his options are sorry ones."

"Aye. Ye are right in that, Riana." Aila gathered her items and removed them to a wooden box in her area of the roundhouse. "Watch over him for a bit, will ye? I'd rather no' speak to the man. Ye can break the bad news to him if he wakes."

Riana cut her a sidelong look as she disappeared behind her own sleeping curtain. For as much as she loved her sister, leave it to Aila to get out of the dirty work, delegating it to Riana. Though 'twas a nasty trick, Riana was used to it. Between her father, stepmother, and sisters, they oft left the less desirable endeavors to her – the injured Roman notwithstanding.

She stood and nudged the barely conscious man with her toe again.

"Roman, are ye awake? Roman?" She hoped the young soldier spoke a few words of *Gaelig*, otherwise 'twould be a rough several months for the Roman. The man groaned in response.

He tried to say something in his strange language that had too many "us" and "a" sounds. How did one learn such a redundant-sounding language? She squatted to be nearer to him.

"Try again, Roman," she demanded in a hushed tone.

Her eyes flicked around the wheelhouse. Her stepmother reclined behind her partition, as did her other sisters. 'Twas only herself and this man in the dancing light of the hearth. She rubbed her hands over his hair and face in gentle swirls, trying to bring him to life.

He spoke in his language again.

"Ye need to speak the *Gaelig*, Roman. Have ye the tongue?"

"Aye," he croaked, then fell back into oblivion.

Riana sighed against her sleeve. The Roman could no stay in the main house — servants and slaves were housed in their own quarters, and he must be chained. Her father would insist on it. Leaving the man on her pallet momentarily, she stepped outside to the small gathering of her father's men in the yard.

"Would ye please?" She gestured into the depths of the house. "Can ye bring the Roman to a servant's hut? He's been bandaged, but he will need to be chained, if he should wake. Father doesna want the man to escape."

Accustomed to being commanded by the chieftain's oldest daughter, three of the men entered the wheelhouse while a fourth ran toward the blacksmith to claim a set of heavy iron shackles.

Riana hated asking for the shackles, but she had no choice. Other than not chaining him meant going against her father's dictates — the goddesses knew she didn't need any more strife with him — she would never risk the safety of her tribe and kinsmen by letting the enemy run loose. The chains though . . .

The idea of slavery had always left a foul taste in her mouth and a pang in her chest. Even though her father and her tribe as a whole were kind taskmasters, the design of captivity ran against her vein of stubborn independence. Conflict roiled inside her as she watched Niall return with the shackles just as the men exited the house, the Roman draped over their arms.

They dropped him unceremoniously on the dirt floor of the hut, a plume of dust swirling around the poor man. Niall clanked the metal cuff around the Roman's ankles and attached the end link to the bolt on a wooden post against the far wall. The men left wordlessly.

Riana made to follow, stopping at the door to gaze back at the broken, unconscious man lying in the dirt. Had he any idea that morning, when he woke, that his life would take such a dramatic turn? That his freedoms would lead to captivity? That today was his last day as a free man? Shaking her vermilion head to dispel such dire thoughts, she left the hut.

The Roman didn't deserve such considerations. He was now only a slave, after all.

~~~

When he woke, his arm throbbed in cadence to the pounding in his head, but at least his arm was still there. After the spear took a chunk from him, Horatio thought he might lose it.

Reaching his good right arm around, he felt the bandage wrapped taut against his skin. It seemed the person who treated his arm possessed a modicum of skill, so they, whoever *they* were, didn't want him dead. He could take moderate comfort in that.

He cracked his eyes open. The light was dim, but through an opening in the thatched roof, Horatio could see several faint rays of daylight filter through narrow gaps. He'd slept through the night, then. Maybe two?

Where am I? Does my contingent know I'm gone?

He tried to sit up, but the pounding in his head forced him back down on the thin pallet that served as his bed. A clanking noise drew his attention, and he flicked his sore eyes to his ankles, which were tethered to a post at the edge of the room.

What?

Now he was wide awake. Why was he chained? Was he a prisoner? He struggled to recall the events of the previous night.

He was bare to the waist, and his own leg coverings had been replaced by rough, loose leggings. And his skin was smooth, clean. Not only was his arm treated, someone bathed him. Why did they bathe a prisoner?

His aching brain tried unsuccessfully to make sense of his predicament when a stunning red-haired woman stepped into the room. For a moment, Horatio lost his senses.

At first, he thought her the result of a fevered dream — no one on earth looked as she did. That hair, a chaotic mass of wavy tresses as vibrant as Opimian wine. Sharply defined bones of her face, milky pale skin tinted with faint blue lines across her forehead, and a voluminous patterned cape that she somehow had tucked into her belt over her gown, similar to the *stolas* women wore in the Empire. Her cape flowed in billowing curves that granted her a commanding presence as she entered the room, and under the neckline, a gold torc circled her slender neck. She was brighter than the sun, too striking to look at for long. Who was this woman? Where was he?

"Where am I?" he asked in his familiar, formal Latin.

The woman didn't answer, silent as the night as she set a platter before him — what appeared to be dried fish and a boiled egg. Not an emperor's feast.

"Latin?" he asked as he sat up. Most of the Empire spoke Latin, including vanquished peoples and those almost conquered. The woman's pale green stare bore into his face, and the blue lines on her brow creased. So, no Latin then.

Other soldiers had taught him a smattering of the language of these northern people — a bizarre, throaty way of speaking that reminded him of growling wolves.

"*Gaelig*," the red-haired woman answered in her tinged dialect.

Horatio nodded in return to convey his understanding.

"Where am I?" he asked in her language.

His eyes searched the interior of the room. 'Twas more of a hut, a small round house with a cold, unused hearth in the center, a pot to one side, and a low door across from where he reclined on the ground. *Spartan* was a compliment.

"Kilsyth," she answered, leaning over his lap to investigate his wound.

She rested her hand on his chest for leverage, and Horatio was quite shocked at her boldness. The woman was so close, her hair tickled his face.

"Where is that?" he probed. She certainly wasn't forthcoming with information.

"Caledonii," was all she said, flicking him with a hard gaze, and a chill crept across his spine.

The Caledonii? The wild men north of Antoine's Wall? How did he get here? He had crossed the army perimeter on a stupid dare from that dandy soldier, Serge, after far too many drinks of stale wine, and once over, he'd floundered around to find a place to piss. 'Twas darker in the tree line than he realized, and he couldn't figure out which direction led back to his contingent. Who knew how long he had stumbled around the woods, drunk and lost. Horatio didn't. He'd been searching for the trail when a sharp strike of pain exploded in his arm.

What had happened that he should awake in a Caledonii hut? As a Caledonii prisoner? There was supposed to be a peace treaty . . .

Horatio moved to sit up further, and the scarlet woman placed her hand flat on his chest.

"Dinna move. I'm trying to check your arm and your head."

She spoke slowly, so he managed to understand her well enough. Her breath was warm in his ear, and had Horatio been in any other situation, he might have panted with excitement. In his present pained state, chained to a post and his future unknown, 'twasn't passion that rose within him. 'Twas fear.

The Maiden of the Storm

Tamping that rising panic down as he'd been taught in his training, he remained still, letting the red woman peer at his wounds. She then sat back on her heels, pushing the platter of food closer.

"Eat," she told him as she rose to leave.

"Wait!" he called out, grabbing at her skirts. Her severe gaze cut at him as sharp as a knife. "What am I doing here?"

If he weren't so distraught and trying to recover from injury, Horatio might have thought he saw a twitch of softening in her pressed lips. Then her grimace returned, and as it was, he must have imagined the tender look.

"Ye will await my father. Chieftain Ru will tell ye what is to be done with ye."

She yanked her skirts from his hands and departed, leaving Horatio alone with his food and his thoughts.

∽

Bronwyn and Maeve met her just outside the worn door. Pale sunlight graced them with its presence, and Riana smiled at her sisters, shades of dark and bright. Maeve, Riana's younger sister by only a couple of summers, resembled all of Ru's children — every hue of red hair and green eyes. Nary a difference among them.

Bronwyn, in comparison, adopted as a wee bairn only a few months old, was of the deepest midnight, with middy skin and shiny tresses blacker than onyx. She exuded mystery.

But the two girls were best of friends, and rarely did Riana see Bronwyn without Maeve by her side.

"What of the lad?" Bronwyn asked in her subdued voice. Never had the lass been the excitable sort.

Then there was Maeve.

"Yes, Riana! Don't make us wait! Tell us about him!"

Maeve seemed younger than her seventeen summers as she jumped up and down in the patchy grass. A matronly smile crossed Riana's face at her sisters.

"'Tis naught to tell. He woke, spoke a smattering of poor *Gaelig*, and I left him to his own devices. And he's a man, not a lad. Just a very lean man."

Bronwyn and Maeve exchanged a startled look. In a tribe of men built larger than mountains, any man of a slender build must certainly be a lad. Or sickly. They giggled together at the prospect.

"If ye claim it so," Bronwyn commented.

"Did he say where he's from? Or what he was doing to get caught?"

Riana shook her head. Their father had not been forthcoming, either. Why was he insistent on keeping a Roman as a slave? The more she pondered his predicament, the more it concerned her. 'Twas not their way to keep Roman soldiers, tensions high with that army as 'twas. She may be a woman, but her father and his men still spoke freely around her, and she wasn't a fool. Anyone in the tribe knew what dangers the Romans wrought. Why keep an icon of such evil here in the camp?

"I will tell ye what I ken when I learn of it. For now, get ye about your chores. I am sure people are hungry and want to eat?" She waved her sisters away.

They turned and retreated from whence they came, still giggling, but with much heavier feet. The prospect of chores was never a joyous one. And undoubtedly less interesting than conversing with the stranger in the hut.

Riana paused before heading off to her own set of chores, flicking her eyes at the wooden door once more. The Roman was a strange man indeed. His size, so much leaner than the men of the Caledonii, gave him a youthful appearance, as did his skin that resembled her father's when he spent too much time shirtless in the sun. Bronzed, like a piece of jewelry or a statue. His hair and eyes were of the earth as well — his hair the rich color of soil after a rain and his eyes mottled to resemble the knotty pine of the mighty Aspen. In truth, he was everything a Caledonii man was not.

And to her surprise, Riana found him intriguing beyond measure.

∽

Horatio's second meal of the day came as sunlight departed the opening in the thatched roof. Though the hut was more or less ramshackle, ready to blow away with the least wind, it must be sturdier than it appeared if it housed captives. And the posts were deeply set in the ground and the stones near the foundation — his tugging on the post was ineffectual and tiring.

And it made his injured arm ache. He poked at it several times as he considered his present circumstances. His regiment must now know he was missing. While they had grown less formal since their contingent had departed from Rome, his friends Marcus or Julian surely must have reported his absence to their commanding Prefect.

His situation seemed dire, especially since he was uncertain about what his immediate future held. Horatio chose instead to focus on his fortunes thus far.

He supposed he was fortunate that he lived at all. 'Twas his own foolishness, taking a drunkard's dare to piss on the other side of the camp and get lost as he did so. These Caledonii weren't necessarily known for their peaceful ways, and that spear could have just as easily pierced his heart as it did his arm.

And 'twas in his favor that winter had shed its frigid skin and the warmth of summer was upon them, given as he wore nothing but a loose pair of trews. His tunic, leather jerkin, and his weapons were gone, probably into the hands of a northern barbarian. Even his meager shoe-boots had disappeared. Then he realized another piece of his good fortune — he'd left his tattered but treasured *sagum* cloak behind with his men. These Caledonii couldn't take that.

The bandage wrapped around the injury bothered him. He wanted to find a blessing in it — that they treated it well and perchance pus might not set in. Yet, if they were looking to kill him, why care for his wound? A festering apprehension, one more harrowing than anything the wound on his arm could produce, rose from the pit of his wame and caused a wave of burning vomit to form in the back of his throat. He choked it down.

Armies didn't treat the injured of their enemies. They let them bleed to death in the fields. If these northerners wished him dead, he would be dead. No, they wanted him for something else.

'Twas on the heels of that notion when the rickety door banged open, announcing the entrance of one of the largest men Horatio thought ever to walk the earth. A bright crimson wild man, without a doubt, a Caledonii with blue and red lines painted above his thick russet-brown beard, could have been a Titan from the old stories. Though he tried not to, Horatio found himself cowering in the man's presence.

Following him, another Caledonii, another wild man of a similar build but less imposing and with only a shadow of a beard, entered the room, keeping a sword near Horatio's head. Two women came after him, obviously sisters. One was the same strikingly beautiful woman who'd brought him his earlier meal.

The Maiden of the Storm

The other girl, a bit shorter than the bright woman, crouched at his side and set a bowl of water and a small animal-fur sac on the dirt next to him. With the sword resting alongside his cheek, Horatio understood he wasn't to move and allowed the other lass to poke about his arm wound. He was close enough to note her hair, bound under a head-covering, appeared to be a few shades lighter than her sister's. Her hands were wrapped in strange bandages, though they didn't seem injured.

After reapplying more paste and re-wrapping the wound, this sister turned to the giant, nodded her head, and retreated from the hut.

The giant's piercing stare sent a shiver of dismay down Horatio's spine. This man must be the chieftain that the woman had mentioned earlier. Now was the moment of truth — he would learn his fate.

"My daughter says ye speak the *Gaelig*?" He spoke in tones even lower than Horatio imagined and growled as any wolf. Horatio strained to comprehend his words.

"Aye," Horatio answered, trying to keep his voice strong despite his dread. "I speak some *Gaelig*."

The giant nodded. Horatio flicked his gaze at his stunning visitor from earlier, but she kept those peridot eyes averted.

"Ye ken where ye are?" the giant asked.

Horatio tipped his head slowly.

"That woman said ye are Caledonii. North of the wall?"

The giant spat on the ground near Horatio, who flinched away with disgust and a modicum of insult. Why was he getting spit at by this northerner?

"Your wall. Much good as it did ye." The giant pursed thick lips that disappeared under his beard. "Ye and yours, ye Romans, even in peace, so much as 'tis, ye keep trying our patience. On our land, eating our fruits and animals, thieving what ye think is yours."

The Maiden of the Storm

The giant knelt on the ground, putting his heavy face across from Horatio's. Hot breath from the chieftain's heady breathing filled his senses. The man moved easily for such a giant; his girth didn't hinder his movements.

"I am tired of ye Romans. I had decided that the next one we saw, we wouldn't kill. Nay, we would play your terrible game of slavery. Stories of Roman slavery is kenned far and wide, aye?"

The blood in Horatio's body froze. A prisoner, that he could understand. Soldiers were taken as prisoners all the time, then used for ransom. But enslaved? Removed from his world, his station, and forced to serve these barbarians for the rest of his life? To live at their mercy? Not to be ransomed back?

The Romans practiced slavery — 'twas well known. But as a soldier, he was supposed to have protections. He was too proud to be a slave! He was . . .

A smack to the side of his head brought his attention back to the giant.

"Do ye understand my words?"

Horatio couldn't answer, his jaw as frozen as the rest of him. The behemoth chieftain shifted his fierce scrutiny to the lass standing by the doorway.

"Roman," she called out in her softer brogue as she studied the dirt floor. "My father has asked ye if ye understand ye are to be a slave here and serve the people of the Caledonii as directed."

The lass spoke to him, yet her eyes didn't rise to meet his. Was she shamed at this circumstance? Did she disagree with her father's decision?

Horatio held the woman in his sights for several erratic heartbeats before looking back at the giant.

"Aye," he answered in a low voice. "I understand."

The chieftain nodded to those gathered in the hut, then they turned and exited, ducking out the low doorway.

"But you will not keep me here," Horatio promised in a Latin whisper heard only by himself.

Chapter Three: Won't They Come for Him?

"FATHER."

Riana halted Ru as he made his way back toward the wheelhouse for his own meal of boiled mutton and thick black-barley bread that her stepmother would have waiting for him. So unlike Riana, the second wife, Tege, looked just as her name indicated — a pretty little thing, with soft, dark blonde waves and no voice. 'Twas probably the reason Ru took her for his second wife.

Often, either in anger or appreciation, Ru commented that Riana was too much like her beloved mother, who died after their youngest sister, Sloane, was born. A difficult birth after four easy ones, and her death had devastated the village. From what Riana could remember and later heard about her mother, she'd had a tongue that could vanquish the fiercest harpy.

In the gloaming this night, 'twas anger that Riana roused in Ru.

"What ails ye now, Riana?" He didn't even try to hide his exasperation with his oldest child.

"I ken we keep slaves. 'Tis the way of our people. Of all the world. Yet, 'twould seem ye are inviting danger keeping this Roman as a slave. The Romans have tried to invade us again after years of peace. Why antagonize them? Won't they come for him?"

Ru sighed heavily, his aggravation at his oldest daughter's contrary nature rising beneath his skin.

"I ken ye are worrit, lass. Your concerns are nay without merit. But the Romans have no' stopped. Perchance 'tis time to change our tactics."

Riana couldn't argue her father's claim for tactics. He was known throughout the Caledonii tribes as a brilliant tactician, with the blood of King Gartnaith Blogh running through him. 'Twas a combination that had served her father well.

However, they weren't at war with the Romans here in Kilsyth. And Riana feared her father's inability to see that may end in disaster.

"Get ye on with your chores. Bring Niall or another guard with ye when ye retrieve the Roman's meal from now on. I shall set him in your and Aila's care. Give him a few days to heal, then give him work. A lot of it. As a soldier, he is young and hale and hardworking. He should prove useful to our tribe."

Again, her father had the right of it, and the commanding tone of his voice told her that he was done discussing the Roman with her.

Instead of answering with a tart retort, she curbed her tongue. Riana gave Ru a slight bow, knowing when she had been dismissed, and made her way back to the hut where Niall stood guard.

"I shall only be a moment to retrieve the platter. If I have need of ye, I shall call out," she told the young Caledonii.

Niall placed his arm across his broad chest and bowed from the waist. Then he swept his arm to the door, holding it open for her.

Lifting her woolen, hunter-green skirt, Riana stepped lightly back into the room.

The Roman had finished eating, what little he did eat, and pushed the platter to the side. Now he sat in the dirt, his legs pulled up against his chest and his head hanging between his knees. He was the image of despondency.

As the high-born daughter of a chieftain, she couldn't imagine what 'twas to be brought so low. Did he have a family? Shall someone, other than his army, miss him?

"Are ye quite finished?" she asked politely.

The Roman didn't answer, so she walked over and retrieved the tray from the ground.

"Ye will nay survive if ye dinna eat," she admonished, noting one bite of cheese and a few berries were not enough to sustain even his lean frame. For men of her tribe, 'twas the start of a snack.

"Do ye think I care?" he mumbled from between his knees.

"No' right now. But ye may care in the future. 'Tis a waste of food. Ye dinna want to receive a flogging for so minor an offense as not eating. Or for your inability to work because ye are starving yourself."

That dark, short-haired Roman head didn't move.

Riana huffed and gathered her skirts to sit across from him. She lay a gentle hand on his arm.

"We are nay cruel people, Roman," she told him in a tender tone. "We dinna starve our slaves. We dinna beat them without cause. Ye shall be well cared for, with warm clothing and footwear. Ye shall fare well here."

A sad promise, but 'twas the only words she had to offer.

He muttered something, and she strained to hear him. "What?"

The Roman lifted his head sharply, his amber eyes cutting into hers. When he spoke, his voice was robust, not at all reflective of the despondent man before her.

"Horatio. My name is not *Roman*. 'Tis Horatio."

'Twas like he was daring her to know his name, know he was more than a mere possession.

"Horatio," she pronounced the strange name slowly.

It stumbled from her mouth in an awkward affectation. He pursed his parched lips at hearing his name spoken thusly.

"I am called Riana."

"Riana," Horatio repeated. "The daughter of the king."

An inappropriate laugh bubbled inside her, and she failed to keep it contained. One slick, earthy eyebrow rose at her reaction.

"He's nay the king, Ro — *Horatio*," she caught herself. "He's distant kin, a close confidant to the king, but he's the Caledonii chieftain of this village. I'm a chieftain's daughter."

"Oh, a lowly woman then," he said, surprising himself at the joke that fell from his lips.

Horatio watched as a grin tugged at her delicate cheek, and when she smiled, 'twas as if the sun parted the clouds and was shining just for him. He shook his head in a painful move, trying to dislodge that thought. She saw him as a slave, not a soldier. 'Twas not his place to dally. She was not a woman who would ever be a conquest.

Nay, she'd be the one wielding the whip if they found him misbehaving.

Horatio stiffened, pulling away from her in a conscious act to protect himself. Riana noticed his discomfort and wiped the smile from her face. *Like the sun went behind the clouds,* he thought briefly before he shook off the notion.

"I will leave the cheese with ye. And the *quaich* of water. Rest, heal. The pot over there is to relieve your needs. And a guard will stand outside your door every night. I will return with Aila in the morn with more vittles and to check your wound. Try to sleep. Ye shall only have a few days before ye are put to work."

Horatio turned those somber eyes back to his knees. Riana waited a moment, pitying the broken man before her, before leaving the hut.

Niall waved her off as she made her way to the washing bucket outside the wheelhouse to wipe the platter clean before setting it on the shelf in their kitchen area. The late spring sun had just set when she entered, and the curtain to her father's sleeping pallet was pulled closed. She would have no more conference with him this night, and for that she was grateful.

Aila and Maeve ate at a low table near the center of the house, their own platters laden with stringy mutton and hunks of half-eaten black bread.

Maeve's face lit up when Riana brought over her own trencher, including a few hardy berries drizzled with honey to appease her sweet tooth.

"What did ye learn?" Maeve pried.

Now in the company of her sisters, Riana relaxed and let her smile shine. Aila and Maeve leaned in, an eager audience.

Riana waited until she finished chewing her boiled meat before speaking.

"His name is Horatio," she told them. Her sisters' smiles matched her own. "But other than that, he told me naught. He's a bit demoralized, aye?"

The women at the table grew solemn at Riana's words. A novelty the man may be, he was still a man who didn't take well to imprisonment.

"He's handsome enough," Maeve observed. "Mayhap he can serve in other ways."

Aila and Riana blushed in a matching deep rose at Maeve's bawdy suggestion. She was always one to try and shock.

"Either way," Riana said, dismissing Maeve's tease, "the lad must rest for another day or two before he begins his work. When Aila decides his arm is healed."

"From what I can see thus far, the wound is no' pink, and no pus has started to appear. If he keeps like this for another two days, he should be ready to work."

"What will he do?" Maeve asked.

"Whatever father demands of him," Riana said with authority.

ॐ

Dunbraith emerged from the shadows of the roundhouse, catching Ru unawares. Ru cursed under his breath — the man was slippery, appearing when least expected.

"I canna abide how the lass speaks to ye. As her father, as the chieftain in this tribe, Riana should speak to ye with more respect." Dunbraith spat on the ground by his feet.

Ru shrugged him off.

"I ken your concerns. But she was raised as a leader, and she wears the mantle of the chieftain's daughter well. I prefer that I have a sturdy lass, one who does no' fear confronting me, than a spineless lass who cowers."

Dunbraith made a rough noise in the back of his throat, letting Ru know what he thought of *that* idea.

"She does speak up, 'tis for certain."

"Accountability is an agreeable thing, Dunbraith. Oft a man canna see something the way he should. Men get too caught up in their own perceptions. Just as ye advise me, so does Riana. Only, her perspective is strangely different than yours or mine. I dinna ken if 'tis her age, or her sex, or the fact she's my daughter."

"Her vehemence over the Roman worries me, Ru," Dunbraith explained.

Ru nodded.

"I, too, fear she may do something drastic regarding the Roman. As of yet, she has been naught but an obedient daughter. And when the sun sets, I ken *that* to be true. I trust her implicitly. She is her father's daughter and will do what is best for the tribe."

Dunbraith nodded, but his gesture was a lie. Women in particular, Dunbraith believed, when their emotions got the better of them, they acted in impulsive and devastating ways. While he didn't say as much to Ru who had six daughters, Dunbraith wondered if the lass might not be the obedient daughter Ru presumed her to be.

He bid Ru good eve and flipped the hood of his plaid *breacan* over his head against the misty night air. Ru was a strong chieftain, a great chieftain, kin to the King, and a loyal friend. But he was jaded by his love for his daughters, and Dunbraith knew deep in his soul that Ru's blindness to his daughter would eventually give rise to a catastrophe.

Dunbraith had studied such things with one of the last remaining *druidai* when he was a young man.

And that catastrophe may well come sooner rather than later.

⁓

Horatio spent bored days drawing on the dirt floor with his finger. His arm throbbed less, which gave his brain time to be idle. Eat the meals, piss in the pot in the corner, draw in the dirt. Nap, if he was tired. The existence was dull beyond measure, but 'twas a fair sight better than death or working his hands to the bone. He supposed he should be grateful for this slow time whilst he had it. 'Twould be gone too soon.

The only bright spot of his day was the enchanting, brilliant woman who brought his meals. She was unlike anyone he'd encountered in all his short life. These Caledonii were a strangely colored people, many of them topped with wild swaths of hair in every shade of russet to sunrise. Coupled with their light eyes, blues, greens, the colors of the Mediterranean, like the view from the hills of his Grecian home, they were walking murals in human form.

Even their size. As a whole, they were giants. Other than his one encounter with a Germanic tribe on his travels north, he'd not met any humans who grew to such heights. Or girths. While she was tall for a woman, Riana wasn't overly tall, but her build! The woman was all bosom and hips, and Horatio had to work to keep his cock from revealing his thoughts, even while shackled. What manner of woman had the power to make a man rise when iron manacles weighed him down?

Other than her name and position in this tribe, he knew nothing of her.

Horatio vowed to remedy that with her next visit.

When she arrived with the evening meal and her sister, who bore a striking resemblance but somehow lacked Riana's captivating appeal, he bided his time. With extreme patience, he waited while Riana's sister, wrapped in her bizarre swaths of fabric, poked and prodded and pasted. Once she gave his arm a gentle pat, the sister gathered her skirts and departed.

The brilliant woman, Riana, set the platter before him, this time presenting a feast of dried eel and beef, another hunk of cheese, and a dry, dark brown bread. Typical of her previous behavior, she sat across from him and cast her pale green gaze upon him, waiting for him to finish eating.

"How many sisters do ye have?" Horatio asked around a mouthful of cheese and bread. His curiosity about her piqued every time her image crossed his thoughts.

"Five," she answered. Then silence.

Not a conversationalist, he realized.

"Are they near your age?" He hadn't seen any younger children with her, nor had she spoken of them. The only outside sounds he could discern were of workers and animals.

"Aye. My father's children are grown."

He paused, at a loss. What else could he inquire about her? Anything that might elicit more than short phrase answers?

"Do ye enjoy living this far north?"

He could have kicked himself. *Stupid question.* But what did one ask in conference with one's master? One's comely master?

She must have noted his discomfort. A bright eye squinted at him.

"'Tis all I ken. This place is the only world I have known."

Ahh, more than one word or short phrase!

"Is it always this cool?"

A wide smile split the serious mask she wore.

"Cool? Right now, 'tis most temperate! I dinna even wear my *arasaid*!"

As soon as she spoke, her eyes widened and she clapped her hands over her mouth, covering those pink lips that he so wanted to kiss.

What was wrong with him? How could he have such thoughts about her?

"*Arasaid*?" he asked, trying to focus on something other than her décolletage that shook invitingly when she moved. 'Twas a struggle to keep his eyes on her shining face.

Riana's expression assumed her previously stoic composure. "My cloak? The plaid cape. 'Tis called an *arasaid*. Or the cape men wear, a *breacan*."

"And your men show their bare legs in the chill. If I'd not had my trews this winter, I don't know what I would have done."

He gazed at his dirty feet.

"Speaking of which, will I have my shoe-boots returned? Or will I be expected to work in bare skin?"

The reminder of his position in her tribe sobered them both. Riana nodded gravely.

"I shall locate footwear for ye. If nay your own, then I'll retrieve a pair for ye."

A hushed silence fell over them as Horatio finished his meal. He tried to drag it out, to share as much time with this goddess as he could, but too soon his food was gone and she was rising, removing his tray. He would again be bored and alone.

In a feat of courage, he lay his hand on her cool one.

"Thank you for your care and company. You don't have to stay here with me, and I am grateful for it."

Riana gave him a steady look.

"I can imagine how dull it must be as ye recuperate here. I will endeavor to visit ye longer until ye begin your duties. Help ye learn of our ways."

Horatio returned her look with a thankful smile, a deep dimple creasing his right cheek under his scrub of a beard, then resumed drawing his pictures in the dirt.

~

Riana was breathless when she left the hut. Giving a quick nod to Niall's eager wave as she secured the door, she carried the empty platter toward her roundhouse. Once she was out of the sentry's view, she leaned against the edge of the house, hiding in the shadows. Her breathing was erratic, almost gasping, and she placed her hand on her chest to slow her panting.

What was wrong with her?

Every time she was near the Roman, her heart raced and 'twas difficult to breathe. She wanted to despise him, treat him as the slave he was, but . . .

Riana shook her head, trying to clear it in the gloaming of nightfall. She was determined to set herself against him, steadfast as the mighty oak. What might happen if she dropped her guard around him? Only disaster.

She vowed not to disappoint her father or her tribe that way. Taking in one more cleansing breath, she brushed the remaining crumbs off platter and ducked inside, greeting her stepmother and her sisters.

Riana's sisters occupied themselves in the house, weaving and sewing cloth in anticipation of the autumn season. With such a large family of daughters, *léines*, *arasaids*, and *breacans* were always a need. Thin leather foot coverings, sewn together with leather thongs supplied by Niall's father and his sons (his house was renowned throughout the entire tribe, not just their village, for the finest, most pliable skins), were spread out in the corner of the room, ready for late summer sizing.

A cauldron bubbled over the fire, the scent of venison thick in the air. Dried venison, most likely, and not Riana's favorite. Skipping a bowl of stew, she instead chose a piece of the brown bread and a hunk of cheese for her supper. She'd missed it while attending the Roman.

"What delayed ye?" Tege asked.

Riana sighed. Though she owed Tege respect as Ru's second wife, she thought Tege a nosy and cold mother figure. With no natural borne children, Tege fashioned herself as the birth mother of Riana and her sisters, trying to wipe away the memory of Riana's true mother.

Being old enough to recall her mother well, Riana didn't acquiesce to Tege at all, and actively fought against the woman, reminding her sisters well of their beloved, bright-haired goddess of a mother. Too often while she was in Tege's presence.

Tege, her sensibilities offended, would hunt down Ru, complaining about Riana and her sisters of that and every other possible offense she might invent. Then Ru would demand obeisance and an apology from Riana.

Ru's daughters detested the game they had to play with their father when it came to his second wife. And Riana would bow her head and offer a weak apology, biting her tongue until it bled, and watch her step until the next time she offended the woman. Then the circle would start again.

At least Tege had a gentle hand, mostly for Gwyneth and Sloane's sakes. As the youngest of the sisters, they were most at Tege's side, and if the wife had laid a heavy hand on her sisters, Riana knew full well she may have responded in kind – violence for violence. And it would have taken much more than a lecture from her father and an apology to resolve it.

Riana tried to look at the brighter side. They could have had it worse, as far as mother figures go. And Tege did love Ru, and that went a long way in Riana's opinion.

"The man eats slow," Riana explained.

'Twasn't a complete untruth, as he'd eaten unhurriedly because of his conversation with Riana.

"Weel, dinna cater to the Roman. He's a slave, after all. He should nay keep ye from your duties. Remind him of that when ye next bring him food. When do ye think he'll be ready for work? He should nay be resting like a god upon furs."

The dirt floor is no' exactly furs. Riana sagely kept her thoughts to herself. Instead, she redirected Tege's attention.

"Aila would ken it best. When she tells me the arm is healed, we can start directing him to his labors."

Tege accepted her answer, turning to speak to Aila. Riana took her meager food outside, hoping to dodge more questions and find a moment of peace.

Blinking lights freckled the black sky — shimmering stars reflecting faraway places of the gods and goddesses. She squatted in a grassy area between her roundhouse and the path that led to the main gate. Sealed tight against any possible nuckelavees of the night, the village was quiet, safe, preparing to rest after a busy day. The gentle bleating of goats and sheep filled the air, and she inhaled deeply, cleansing her woes and connecting to the Mother Goddess, Brigid.

In this calm evening air, her meal was a feast, and she took her time listening to the evening sounds before brushing off her skirts and returning home to find her sleeping furs.

And when she finally lay her head to sleep, she hoped her dreams were not filled with images of a Roman with dark hair and flashing eyes.

The Maiden of the Storm

～

The next day, Riana served the Roman's food quickly before skipping out, looking to tend her goats and collect a small basket of early summer cherries for the midday meal. Niall caught up with her as she exited the goat pen.

"Were ye able to learn anything from the Roman? Ye spoke to him long enough yester eve."

Riana averted her pale gaze from Niall's accusing hazel eyes. Had he listened in on their conversation? Who else had noticed the time she'd spent in the hut?

"He wants his shoes." She looked to her goats as she spoke. "He was wondering if he were to work in bare feet. I told him we would find him proper footwear. Can ye help me with that?"

Niall's nearness made her shake under her kirtle. He was powerfully strong, even as a younger man still growing into full manhood. Many a girl swooned at his shoulder-length blond hair that complimented his sun-kissed skin, Riana included. Yet, she sensed something else burned under that skin, something possessive, demanding. He was too young and too reckless for her to entertain any romantic considerations about him.

Riana assumed he cared for her, in his own way. What she didn't know was if that care was a result of her womanhood or for her position as Ru's oldest daughter. Many a tribal leader had requested conference with her father, trying to arrange a marriage. Riana was a fortunate daughter — he had agreed to let Riana pick her future husband — and as she peered at Niall from the corner of her eye, she knew deep in her chest it wasn't he.

The Maiden of the Storm

She'd yet to inform him of her choice. And his youthful desires meant he oft followed her around like a lost pup. He continued to engage her, find reasons to seek her out and compliment her. And while she enjoyed the boyish attentions, flattery always felt grand, the time was approaching when she must tell him that he wasn't her choice.

She decided to do that when her father was nearby, just in case his possessive underpinning reared its ugly head.

"My father surely has a few old foot coverings lying about our house. I can bring them to ye on the morrow. Will he be working by then?"

Niall stepped closer to her — the heat from his chest blazed through her thin blue *léine*. She should probably step away, but again, there was something comfortable about Niall and his attention. And he didn't press his claim any further, so she remained still, soaking in the light of his clandestine affection.

"Aila would be the better one to ask. I canna think why he would no' be ready, from what I have seen. She did say his wound is healing well."

"Do ye ken where he will work?"

Riana shrugged. So many had asked her that over the last day. She tried not to care what role the Roman might fill. Fanning flames at the smiths? Shoveling goat and sheep waste? Farming? Skinning? Who was she to guess? Her father would make that decision, and Riana had no desire to be a part of that.

"Father will decide. Ye can speak with him." A breeze kicked up, blowing loose tendrils of her vermilion waves across her face. She turned to Niall, tugging the curls out of her eyes. "Are ye nay guarding him?"

Niall shook his beautifully chiseled head. "Eian is on duty with the lad now. Not that a guard is needed. The man is built like a lass."

Niall laughed to himself, and Riana had to bite her tongue. 'Twas dreadful enough the man was chained. Must he be mocked as well?

She twitched her head to focus. The Roman surely would endure more than mocking now that he was a slave of the Caledonii. Best she not meditate on it.

"I must attend my duties, Niall," she said, shifting to move past him. Niall angled himself to allow her to pass. Riana smiled to herself. There — that 'twas why she didn't mind his overeager attempts. He never overstepped. He may have wanted more than friendship, but he was a good friend indeed.

"Good day to ye, Niall," she added as she walked toward the oat fields.

"And to ye, Riana," he answered, his eyes watching the sway of her hips as she sauntered away.

～

Aila joined Riana again that evening when she brought a simple supper to the Roman. *Horatio*, her mind added unwillingly.

Aila poked and prodded as Horatio sat, a bored expression on his face. She declared him healed and ready to resume work. Gathering her poultices, she left Riana alone with the Roman.

His chains jingled as he moved to the platter of food.

"What manner of work will I be starting on the morrow?" he asked as he ate.

Riana pursed her lips.

"I dinna ken. Ye are under the purview of my father. He'll decide what to do with ye and tell the guards."

He scanned his eyes around the interior of the hut.

The Maiden of the Storm

"I don't hear much outside. Some animals and few people. Is there a need for slaves here?"

And he truthfully didn't know where "here" was. Was this the type of place where the ruler lived far from the commoners? Was the village very small? Or was his meager shack far from where most of the tribal people lived?

Riana cut her suspicious eyes to Horatio. It seemed a strange query, and she wondered if he was trying to obtain information from her. *Information he could use to escape?* Her father would scold her severely, physically punish her even, if she gave the Roman what he needed to flee. She didn't answer his question.

He finished chewing, then looked at her with an expression of mild surprise.

"No talking today? Did I say something wrong?"

She shook her head, her wild locks flowing around her shoulders.

"Oh, no fraternizing with the servants. I understand." He grabbed the rest of the food off the platter and held it aloft. "Here's the platter so you can leave."

Riana stared at the tray. Her inner self was more amiable sort and wanted to take part in his friendly banter, but the underlying danger of doing so rang in her head. She took the platter from him, lifted her skirts, and left the hut.

Straining to listen beyond the door, Horatio overheard muffled speech, 'twas all. So much for finding a sole friend in this strange land.

Horatio understood the red goddess's dilemma. Riana may have enjoyed their conversation the day before, but she also must have realized the inherent danger in offering any manner of friendship to him. If he did find a way to escape, she may well be accused of aiding him.

That didn't mean he wouldn't stop trying. If he smiled enough, was friendly enough, perchance she might speak to him again, and he wanted to learn as much about this community as he could.

His destiny would not remain in chains.

Chapter Four: Laws of the Land

AFTER THE RED woman brought his morning meal, one of the young sentries outside the hut, a stocky blond man he'd heard Riana call Niall, entered with another man who was taller and not quite as thick.

The darker-haired man stood by the doorway as Niall withdrew a key from a leather pouch at his waist and unlocked the chains binding his legs to the pole. The Caledonii didn't unlock the irons from his ankles.

"Rise," Niall commanded, and Horatio realized they expected him to walk with his feet shackled. Work with his feet bound.

He muttered a silent curse. That would make running away difficult.

Niall clasped Horatio by his upper arm and yanked him to his feet when Horatio didn't get up fast enough. Stumbling in his chains, he followed Niall to the door.

The sunlight outside was much like every day he'd spent in the northern land thus far, gray with rain-threatening clouds. He blinked against the light nonetheless, his first time back in daylight after his time healing inside the hut.

As Horatio's eyes adjusted, his jailers walked him toward the village gate which was slightly ajar.

No moment like the present, Horatio thought, without a plan or premeditation. While Niall was distracted, looking ahead, Horatio jumped on his toes, banging his head against the Caledonii's with a resounding crack.

He knew the minute the Caledonii fell that the other guard would be on his back in a heartbeat. Anticipating well, Horatio spun and clasped his hands, bringing them up in a solid arc that caught the darker-haired Caledonii under his chin, knocking him to the ground.

Having the element of surprise was always a sound military tactic, but now they knew he was trying to escape, so he had to move fast.

The chains at his ankles, however, hobbled him more than he realized.

He didn't make it five steps before the blond warrior jumped him from behind, his solid mass hitting Horatio as hard as a stone wall and crushing him into the soft earth.

With Horatio pinned in the dirt, Niall pummeled him, raining hammer-like fists to his head and back with wild barbarity. Horatio tried his best to cover his face from the hits, wondering if he made it this far only to be beaten to death by an enraged Caledonii.

The barrage of blows abruptly ceased, and when a dazed Horatio dared a look from under his hands, he saw the other young man hauling Niall off his back.

"Nay, Niall!" the other Caledonii yelled. "Ru does no' want him dead!"

Niall shoved the dark-haired man away and spat on the ground next to Horatio's head. His friend's words finally permeated his skull.

"Get ye up, Roman," Niall bit out. "We'll try this again. And if ye attempt another false move, ye will lose more than a sliver of skin from your head. Chieftain's orders or no'."

The Caledonii seething with fury convinced Horatio of the truth of his words. He'd had his opportunity to flee, and now 'twas gone. This Caledonii would not be caught unawares by Horatio again.

Blood from his forehead dripped into his eye, and Horatio wiped at it with his palms, then wiped his hands on his pants. Horatio stood on shaky legs, the chains at his ankles clanking in a mocking laugh, and waited for the men to resume their path to wherever they were taking him.

He hung his head low as they walked to a stone-ridden field, the burden of his failed escape weighing on his shoulders like the rocks under his feet.

They worked him like a beast of burden. He'd been in the Roman army for several years; training and marching had built strong, lean muscles and fair endurance, but this level of labor was staggering.

First, where did all these rocks come from? Lifting boulders seemed the most banal of any sort of work, yet it tore at his body, wearing out every last muscle, and his bruises from the fight with Niall only made him ache even more. When he lay on his thin pallet that night, his body screamed in agony. It hurt to breathe, and his stomach pinched in hunger.

His mind recalled Riana's caution at his uneaten first meal. She'd been correct in his need for nourishment.

Was this how these northern Celts grew so large? Generations lifting and moving stones? He'd seen their mysterious stone circles — heard tales of their usage as places of magic and sacrifice. Many of those boulders stood taller than Horatio. Had these men moved those enormous stones into place?

He'd learned from other soldiers these Highlander Celts also threw trees and gigantic hammers. Was their only occupation lifting the heaviest things they could find? His mind was the only muscle that didn't hurt, and it churned with these dark thoughts regarding his captors.

Horatio didn't move when Riana entered in a swirl of color and feminine beauty. She was a moment of bright reprive in his miserably arduous day. Now that he'd been put to work, assuming his new, degrading status no better than a beast of burden, Horatio commanded his brain and body to focus on leaving and not let this woman distract him.

Oh, but that was a more difficult task than he'd imagined. She was distraction embodied. He'd never reacted to a woman this way. *Never.* Why now when his life depended so much on keeping his mind on his goal? Why did he lose control now?

Escape.

That was where his focus needed to be. How to find his way back to his contingent. Though he despised the idea of it, if he could use the woman, no matter how his body reacted to her presence, he would. A mighty Roman soldier would not fall so far as to retain this lowly status.

The swifting sound of her skirts as she approached him broke the evening silence. Horatio's breaths, already shaky and shallow from his day's exertions, thinned further, catching as he kept his eyes closed and tried not to envision her graceful movements, the flow of her gown over her hips, her milky neck that led to . . .

Stop! he ordered himself. If he continued his thoughts beyond that, the one remaining muscle he hadn't used today might rise, and how would that appear to Riana?

The sounds in the hut diminished. Horatio waited in his prone position for a few more moments. Had she left?

"I ken ye are nay asleep," Riana said aloud. So, she hadn't exited yet. "I brought ye the evening meal. I'll leave it with ye, but Niall will most likely retrieve it soon, and he'll take the food with it if ye dinna eat quickly."

"Thank you." His words were little more than a rush of air.

He cracked an eye open to see her standing by the door. She gave him a curt nod and departed.

Only then did he move, every muscle screaming as he did so, and grab the hunk of boiled meat off the plate.

⁂

"Ye dinna have to go in there," Niall told her as she stepped out of the low doorway.

She turned toward him, her face clearer than the moon that tried to hide behind the night clouds. Horatio's face had been an unmistakable mess of bruises, and Riana's blood boiled, wanting to chastise Niall for his harsh treatment of the Roman.

The Maiden of the Storm

But to what end? Her words would fall on deaf ears – Niall and the rest of the village cared naught for an injured slave. And she hated sending Niall into the hut to retrieve the tray. It sickened her.

Instead, she looked away, hiding her emotion. Niall's eyes studied her as she spoke.

"I do appreciate the offer, Niall. And if ye could retrieve the platter for me when he's done, 'twould be fine. But since I have to prepare the vittles for him anyway, 'tis of little consequence."

Niall nodded, understanding her commitment to her father's newest acquisition. They'd had few slaves as of late, since the tribes had banded together to fight off the Roman invasion. Though not needed, as the Highland Caledonii men and women were more than capable and strong enough to support their villages and kin, having an extra pair of hands at the cost of a bit of food was welcome.

The pained expression on Riana's face, however, was not. Niall nudged her as she made to walk the short pathway home.

"What ails ye, Riana? Since the man arrived, a shadow has set upon ye."

Her shoulders sagged. Niall read her too well. But she didn't realize 'twas as obvious as he claimed.

"Is it having a slave?" he asked. "I ken we've not had many in your years, but the Caledonii —"

Riana flicked her gaze at the hut.

"Aye. Truth be told, I dinna think I agree with the idea of slaves, Niall. Servants, maybe. They still have freedoms, of a sort. But to take away all virtue of choice from a man? And a Roman soldier no less, who could well bring the wrath of their army to our gates?"

The Maiden of the Storm

She shook her head, pursing her lips at the prospect. "What might ye do, Niall, if ye were stolen from your people? Chained and forced to work, with no chance for any greatness in life? Your very right to live at the mercy of someone else? Nay, even for my enemy, I can no' agree with it."

Niall lay his heavy hand on her arm.

"But 'tis the law of the lands. Many tribes have slaves, and your father has dictated this. Ye would go against him?"

"Nay, Niall. Ye ken me to be my father's daughter. Yet . . ." her voice trailed off, getting lost in the night.

Niall stood straighter, his back stiff and on edge. "What is it, Riana?"

She shook her head again, her mass of russet locks nearly black in the flickering light of the torches.

"'Tis naught. Thank ye, Niall, for the conversation." She graced him with a tight smile. She hadn't forgiven him yet for Horatio's face.

Niall moved swiftly, enclosing her in a brief embrace before releasing her just as quickly.

"I am here for ye, lass, whenever ye need me."

Poor lad, she thought. *He desires a chance at me, my hand, my body.* Unfortunately, nothing inside her burned for him. His touch didn't send shivers across her skin.

"Ye have always been the most steadfast friend, Niall," she acknowledged, hoping he might understand her implication.

If he did, he gave no sign. He bowed his head respectfully.

"Good evening to ye, Riana."

"Ye as well, Niall."

As she picked her way back to the chieftain's wheelhouse, she pondered his embrace. Was that his youthful attempt to show her he cared for her? Or was it something more innocent, one friend consoling another?

The Maiden of the Storm

Riana hoped 'twas the latter.

Chapter Five: What Else Could a Man Want?

THE ROMAN DIDN'T speak to her for days, other than the courtesy of thanking her for food. His amiable behaviors ceased abruptly. The level of work he was doing each day undoubtedly contributed to his quiet nature — exhaustion ate away at him like a parasite, more noticeable each night she brought him his evening meal. Boney ribs poked through his skin, and deep purple half-moons shone from beneath his eyes.

Then she would leave the hut, give Niall a quick nod, and report the Roman's day to her father.

After several days of this silent exchange of meals, the Roman finally spoke.

"Is this all I shall do? Moving rocks? What do you *do* with them?"

His unexpected question caught her by surprise, and she bit back a giggle. The Highlands were renowned for its rocky landscape.

"I mean, I pull them from the ground, move them to a pile, then haul that pile to another just outside the gates, while a scattering of men watches me as they hoe the land, skin a beast, or fell a tree. Why do you need so many rocks?"

Riana set the platter on the ground and sat across from him, spreading her skirts in a comfortable wad around her legs.

"Foundations, aye?" She pointed at the base of the hut. "Roundhouses use them as the base, then we apply daub and wattle on wood stakes for the walls. Then we clear the land for farming, new houses, or animals. And to add to the standing stone circles, as ye've seen in the grove."

"What if I run out of rocks?"

Riana dipped her head, but not before he caught the slender smile that pulled at her full, rosy lips. Did she have any idea how enticing that smile was?

Horatio had tried to ignore her. Keep his eyes closed, focus on the landscape outside as he worked to make mental notes of gaps in their surveillance or when his bindings seemed weak. Concentrate on his goal. But whenever she stepped into the hut, 'twas as if something else took control of his brain, and his mind wasn't his again until she left.

"We have trees to be felled, peat to be collected for fires, thatch to be woven for roofs. And if needed, we can send ye to attend Niall's kin, for slaughtering to prepare leather."

Horatio grimaced, and Riana giggled that mention of the last task got a rise out of him.

"Here," she handed him strips of soft flaxen cloth. He took the fabric, but with a questioning furrow in his brow.

"What am I to do with these?"

"For your ankles."

The Maiden of the Storm

Riana gestured to his feet, where red and swollen welts had formed gaping sores. He grew numb to the pain after a few hours, but the tender skin looked especially afflicted now that the day was over.

"Wrap the strips around the shackles. 'Twill save your ankles and make your chores easier."

Horatio kept his gaze on her face, the gentle lines of her delicate features exuding a sense of kindness he'd not expected. Why was she eager to help him? His golden face flushed in gratitude, and he wrapped the swaths of fabric around the heavy iron manacles.

"I ken this may be a strange question, but are ye settling in well? As best ye can?"

Her query took him aback. What did these Caledonii care if he was well or not? 'Twas not the way of masters to bother overly much about the comfort of their slaves.

"What?" he responded.

Her own smooth brow furrowed, and she tried to make her words more clear. Perchance he hadn't understood her words. "Are ye doing as well as can be expected for a man in your position?"

Horatio's eyebrows rose high on his forehead. He lifted his face to gaze at the worn, thatched ceiling, then to the dirt below his feet, then to his meager supper.

"I have a roof over my head, which is more than I sometimes had as a soldier, a meal every night, and a beautiful woman as my dining companion. And now I have cushion to relieve my ankles. What else could a man want?"

He had tried not to sound too acerbic. Nevertheless, she caught his tone and her smile fled. Her stunning face was once again a mask. Insulted, she rose in a huff.

"I shall leave ye to your meal, then," she said as she spun off toward the door.

At the doorway to the hut, she swirled around to face him once more.

"Your position here is nay my choice, or my doing. I'm following my father's command."

Horatio could only shrug as she departed. Following orders was something he understood well. As a soldier, he was expected to follow a Centauriae's command without question, even when he disagreed with that order.

Could he fault a fair young lass for doing any less for her father?

∽

Riana raced from the hut. Niall's fingertips brushed against her *léine* as she rushed off, but she didn't head toward home. He wanted to follow her, find the source of her ire, but that would leave the hut unguarded. Instead, he watched as she ran off into the night, a red spirit in the mist.

Dealing with her father and stepmother would not help settle the clenching discord in her chest, so she veered to the rear of her house to the gate that led into the animal lean-to. Several smaller beasts were housed in this section of the wheelhouse, which was walled off from the primary living areas with a door for access. At the back, a larger door, little more than a rough wood plank, kept the animals closed in against the night.

The small goats and a few lambs bleated at her interruption but calmed as she combed her hands over their crinkly fur and soft wool, still fluffy until they were sheared after midsummer. Heady scents of manure and hay and animal chased her unease away, clearing her head. The lean-to was one of the best places to find a sense of peace.

It could be anyone, she told herself. Anyone in that hut. No one should be enslaved to another. But especially the young Roman with the lean muscles .. . Guilt and conflict wracked her body.

The sounds of the animals brought her back to her world. She wouldn't go against the dictates of her father, no matter how vile they were. Riana had shared her disagreement with him. That was the norm. And her father did often hear her voice.

This time, though, every word had fallen on unhearing ears. His own sense of vengeance against the Romans was too strong. He saw it as justice — one of the Roman's own enslaved in contrast to the many Celts captured and imprisoned throughout history. And understandable, Riana had to admit.

She just didn't agree with it.

Chapter Six: Questionable Intentions

HORATIO'S SUN-KISSED skin was darker than the Caledonii men's, and that skin was readily apparent as he went about his work stripped to the waist, toting water from the well to the troughs in the village's larger animal barn.

So different in appearance, so glistening and muscled, he turned many a curious village woman's eye as he worked, young and old alike. They giggled and stared at the Roman throughout the day, not bothering to hide their curiosity. Even Riana's sisters joined in, Maeve making her bawdy comments all the while.

Were all Romans that bronzed? Riana wondered, admiring his movements as he went about his labors.

He was leaner, not as full or thick as the Highlanders, rather dense with muscles that flexed and shifted under his dusky skin, showing his strength as he hefted wooden buckets of water from the stone well.

Riana found her eyes watching the mysterious Roman more than she cared to admit, more than she wanted to reveal to anyone, even her beloved sisters. They wouldn't understand her fascination or internal conflict regarding the Roman — no one in her village did. She knew she shouldn't allow herself to become so caught up in the man and his plight. Yet she did.

And in the evening, when she brought his meals, she tried to keep him conversant. Though her initial reaction had been to ignore him, not engage him, her discontent over his position in the tribe won out. He was still a man and deserved a modicum of respect. She wouldn't treat him less than any other man in the village.

"Well, if it isn't my angel with food. What fare have you this eve?"

More than a fortnight of work and bondage hadn't subjugated his personality — his ruddy eyes shone just as brightly at the end of the day of ignoble treatment and harsh labors as it did in the morn. And against her better judgement, she looked forward to that sparkling welcome each evening.

"Ooch, more dried fish, cheese, and bread. I managed to find a small apple for ye, as a treat," she said as she set the platter before him.

Horatio eyed the apple. The ruby orb was as tempting as the one in a story he'd heard from another soldier, about a woman who was kicked out of a garden for such luscious fruit.

Riana's change in her treatment of him had not escaped Horatio's notice. At first, he thought it was just a comfortable nicety, but as of late, her time with him had become more engaging, and he responded in kind. She was the only person in this village who gave him any sort of compassion, spoke to him in something other than a command, and he wasn't going to begrudge that gift.

"The apple is a treat! Thank you." He bowed his head in appreciation.

Riana sat across from him as he ate.

"How long have ye been a soldier?"

She'd grown more relaxed in asking him about his Roman life, and he was only too willing to share. A sense of pride as a soldier, for certain, but who else would converse with him? His engagements with Riana helped break up the drudgery of his days, and she, too, anticipated her time with him. She found herself wanting to learn as much about him as she could.

"Five years. I joined the Roman Legion after I turned twenty. Many boys in my city did. The Legionaries didn't accept them all. Some were too short or not healthy. But most of us who didn't want to be farmers or were second or third sons rallied to the Empire's army."

"Was your family a farming family?"

Riana leaned forward as she inquired, and Horatio had to force his eyes on the shining apple on his tray and not the mounds of swaying breasts that peeked above her gown.

"Aye, and a poor one at that. I send part of my pay to my parents. But even as a young man, I knew I wouldn't be a farmer. I craved something more, to see the world, to be fr —"

He stopped himself, and Riana noticed.

"Free?" Her voice was cautious as she asked. Her heart fluttered in agony at his statement. "You wanted to be free?"

Horatio shrugged. "Many dangers follow the life of a Legionnaire. This is just one of those many."

He said it so matter-of-factly, but Riana didn't believe him — not completely.

The Maiden of the Storm

"And what of you?" Horatio shifted the conversation to something less complicated. "Have you lived here in this village your whole life?"

Riana nodded, a slight smile passing across her face. "I love my sisters, my father, my village. My people are strong. We have traditions and festivals. Truly, unlike ye, I have never wanted to leave. I am quite content in my village."

"I can understand that. You have the benefit of being the daughter of a powerful man. Even in lean times, I am sure you've had plenty. Not to belittle you," he lifted his finely chiseled head, catching her pale gaze. "I would have given much to have a life as ye do."

A heavy, aching sadness welled in her breast at his words. To work so hard to secure freedom, only to have it removed in a harrowing manner.

"Weel, I hope ye dinna find it too cumbersome here," she told him, removing the apple from the platter and placing it in his hand. His fingers lingered on hers, his eyes afire as he stared at her.

"Not with you here," he answered.

His bold response shocked her full force. Riana's heart leapt in her chest, and her blood pounded in her head. She dropped her chin and slipped her hand away. Keeping her gaze at the ground, she grasped the platter and rose quickly.

"Good eve to ye," she said quietly as she exited the hut.

༺༻

"Why do ye do that?" Niall asked her as she stepped from the doorway, ripping her from her thoughts.

Riana spun around at the question, her claret-colored waves dancing over her shoulders. "Do what?"

"Stay in the hut. I can hear ye conversing with the Roman. Ye shouldn't do that. Your father will no' approve. He's not a Caledonii, Riana. Ye should no' treat him as such."

"Dinna lecture me on what I should or shouldn't do, Niall," she told him in a tight voice. The young Caledonii man had no domain over her, regardless of his size or his position in their tribe. She wouldn't allow him to lecture her like she was a child. "He's still a man who deserves a smattering of respect."

"Does he now?" Niall's blond eyebrows rose in disbelief. "Ye are the only one to believe so. To the rest of us, he is less than an animal. His only value is his work. Dinna give him more than that."

"I dinna agree, Niall," she softened her voice, hoping a tender tone might open his ears. "All the Mother's creatures deserve respect."

"Not the enslaved ones," he muttered under his breath before laying his hand on her arm. "I just fear that danger may come to ye if ye spend too much time with this man. He may put your life at risk to attempt an escape. I could never forgive myself if I let anything happen to ye."

Riana patted his hand. She valued the concern that belied his words but didn't want him to think it gave him a claim on her.

"I thank ye for your consideration, but dinna worry for me. I am the daughter of Ru. I can care for myself."

Niall huffed but didn't respond. Riana was wise, but Niall knew she didn't understand what could drive a man to violence, especially against a woman. His face tightened as she lifted his broad hand from her arm.

"Good eve to ye, Niall," she told him as she departed.

She hoped that was the end of his misguided concerns.

And it was, until the next night when Riana was in the midst of assisting Tege at the hearth. When the time came to bring the Roman his meal, Ru tasked Aila with the chore instead.

Riana's eyes cut to Aila, who set the pouches she'd been counting aside and reached for the platter. She kept her gaze averted from Riana. To Riana, it seemed she expected this request.

Had Niall said something to father? she wondered. *Was he gossiping like a crone?* Pretending she didn't hear the command, she continued to poke at the fire, encouraging it to heat so their meat boiled for supper.

Aila gathered a platter of food and left without a backward glance.

∽

"Hello, milady —" Horatio started, then stopped himself as he saw Riana's sister enter the hut.

"Oh, hello," his voice lowered. "Are ye here to check my arm?" He flexed it as he spoke.

The sister hadn't made her presence known in the hut since she last checked on his well-being. The young woman lay the platter on the ground but stood more than an arms-length away.

"Eat your meal. Dinna dally. I am needed at home." She shoved it toward him with her toe.

Horatio scooped the dried meat from the platter and shoveled it into his mouth. The woman's hard face, so unlike Riana's kind features, didn't invite conversation. Thus, Horatio chewed his food and remained silent. Her angry eyes only burned with more ire as he ate. If Riana was the bright spot in this tribe, then this woman was the shadow.

"I dinna ken what ye are thinking with my sister," Aila told him, breaking the hard silence. "If ye attempt to use her as a means to escape. But your life will be forfeit if anything happens to her that's a result of ye or your actions." She snatched the platter away. "Do ye ken my words?"

What manner of man did these people think him to be? And to hurt Riana? She had been the only person in this village to extend him any kindness! He would never risk her safety, even if it meant his freedom. But her family didn't know this. His chest throbbed as these reflections came to his mind and her face danced in his thoughts. No, his actions could never bring danger to her, this he vowed.

Any other person in this tribe, however . . .

A kick to his leg brought his attention back.

"Did ye hear me, Roman?"

Horatio snapped his head up to the woman.

"Yes. I understand."

With a scowl, she nodded once then marched from the hut, leaving Horatio to his ruminations.

What just happened?

※

When Aila returned, Riana approached her, asking after Horatio under the guise of helping her set her packets away.

"Why did ye go to the Roman tonight?" Riana tried to keep the jealous tone out of her voice. Her reaction confused her. Why should she be jealous?

"Niall asked it of me. He was worried that ye were becoming too close with the Roman, that the Roman might use your kindness against ye to flee. I told father that I should give the Roman a check since he's been working, make sure the wound healed completely."

Riana's face hardened at her sister's words. Why did everyone think her so simple-minded that she'd permit the Roman to manipulate her and escape? Or did they think her so weak-hearted she'd help him? Her dislike for slavery was no secret.

"What did ye tell him?"

Aila's eyes remained on her herbals as she spoke. "Naught that he didn't already know. That his life would be forfeit should anything happen to ye."

"What?" Riana's voice rose louder than she expected, and she glanced around to make sure she hadn't drawn attention to herself. Tege and her other sisters sewed by the hearth, their regard for their task unwavering.

"He needs to ken his place, Riana," Aila told her flatly. She raised her flinty green eyes to Riana. "And ye should remember yours. 'Tis a dangerous game ye play with the Roman."

"I dinna play any games," Riana responded, trying to be as honest as possible. "I only give him the same courtesy I give any man in the village."

"I ken ye, Riana. Dinna forget yourself."

"Ye ken naught, Aila," Riana retorted.

Aila didn't answer, only raised one bright red eyebrow. She didn't believe Riana for a minute.

Riana stormed off to her own pallet of furs, fuming. How dare Niall and Aila plot behind her back like that?

The Maiden of the Storm

Niall didn't look at her when she entered the hut early the following morn. Horatio sat, legs bound, his shoulders against the wall. He peeled one eye open when she arrived.

"Milady returns. I missed your company yesterday."

Riana bit the inside of her mouth as she set the tray on the ground.

"So my sister is nay the conversationalist, eh?"

Horatio's defined chest shook as he chuckled at the comment.

"I think you know the answer to that. Regardless, I'm pleased you have returned."

He swiped the bread off the trencher, taking a large bite.

"She told me what she said to ye," Riana told him.

Horatio nodded, swallowing the bread and setting the rest down on the tray. He took her pale hand in his rough, scabbed fingers and caught her eyes with his own. The intensity in his bronze gaze made her breath catch. She wanted to look away, break that gaze, but she couldn't.

"Your sister fears I will force you to help me escape or use you to assist me in that endeavor. I shall have you know that I'll not do such a thing to you. Your courtesies have been the only kindness I have known since I have been brought here. I respect you too much to risk your safety. Please know that to be true."

Riana yanked her hand away. If the man were manipulating her, he was devilishly good at it. At the same time, his words struck a chord deep inside her. She nodded politely, then waited until he removed the rest of his food from the platter before rising to leave.

"Thank ye, for that," she finally answered as she left.

Horatio was sweating later that day, a surprising heat that made him grateful for a lack of a tunic. The leather straps that left blisters on his chest, however, garnered no appreciation.

Village farmers wanted furrows for their early summer plantings, and there weren't enough horses to complete the job. Or they didn't want to use healthy animals in such low work. His blond Caledonii guard, the one called Niall, had offered up Horatio as a substitute.

The bastard.

The blisters popped and peeled, and blood began to run under them, yet he still dug his feet into the fresh earth, pulling the broad blade plow as a fat village farmer followed, balancing it with the wooden handles. The villager made sure to give Horatio several ladles of water throughout the day, but his skin gaped, and muscles ached with every step. Marching miles upon miles had nothing on being on the working end of a plow.

When the sun finally settled low in the sky, Horatio slowed, trying to accommodate his blisters while finishing the row for the villager. Squinting into the dusky late sunlight, Horatio didn't notice the hand that smacked the back of his head until he was reeling on the ground. He shaded his eyes against the sun to see the hairy blond giant, Niall, standing over him.

"What ails ye, Roman? Do ye think to be idle afore your work is done?"

Niall kicked him in the belly to punctuate his question, an unexpected, forceful kick that bruised his stomach and expelled every last bit of air from his lungs. Horatio rolled on his side and supported his weight with his elbow, trying to catch his breath before rising.

The Maiden of the Storm

"What is wrong with ye, Niall?" a second, familiar voice echoed across the farmland.

No, lass. Dinna come to my aid, Horatio thought. Any interference would only cast shadows of doubt and accusations upon Riana.

"He was working! Do ye nay see his chest, the bloody mess 'tis? He does no' need your heavy hand to make it worse!"

"Dinna tell me how to guard my quarry, Riana."

Niall's voice was tight and level. Her intervention struck a chord deep in his wame, and he wasn't about to let her irritate him or anger him in front of the Roman.

"If ye make it worse, he will no' be able to work, ye fool!" she screeched in a high-pitched tone. Riana's ire was beyond elevated. It flew to the sky with the birds.

"Why do ye care, Riana?" Niall caught her arm — not softly or out of concern, but strong, as if reminding her of his power. "'Tis unnatural how ye mind the slave!"

Riana yanked her arm from his grip. Her hair seemed to stand on end, making her look larger than the man she confronted. This time she wasn't going to permit Niall to abuse Horatio.

"If he's injured, he canna work, ye fool. And 'tis a matter of basic respect for one of nature's creatures. I canna abide by such punishments for one of nature's own!"

"Dinna give me some 'goddess' reason," Niall smirked at her.

He smirked! Riana clenched her jaw at him. The Horned God himself would have cast Niall out for his insults.

"Slaves are lower than any of nature's creatures," Niall continued. "He must know his place." This time when Niall grabbed her arm, it hurt. "And 'tis best ye ken yours, Riana."

His last statement was ominous, but Riana dismissed it as he walked away. She rushed to Horatio, who sat mutely in the dirt. He didn't want to imagine Niall's reaction if he had tried to intervene.

The portly farmer crouched down with Riana, another ladle of water in his hand.

"'Tis fine, lassie," the farmer told her as he handed Horatio the cup. "We are quite finished. I'll have the Roman returned to his hut."

Riana nodded, turning her attention to Horatio. Her eyes narrowed at the bloodied blisters. "Aila will accompany me when I attend ye this eve. Your wounds will need to be treated."

Horatio gasped as he tried to drink and breathe at the same time. Then he cut his eyes to Riana.

"'Twould be best if you didn't bring my meal tonight. Send Aila alone. I will not be much for conversation, and I don't think we should give your blond man any more reason for suspicion or violence."

Riana's skin bristled. "He's not my blond man," she spit out.

Horatio finished his water and handed the ladle to the farmer, nodding his thanks.

"You better tell him that," he told her before struggling to his feet.

The farmer and Riana both reached out a hand to help. Horatio turned his back to Riana and was led away by the fat villager.

∽

Her mind was a jumble of confusion.

Niall was a perfectly acceptable, handsome young man of her tribe. He was everything she should want in a man who became her mate. Yet she felt nothing for him, nothing more than the friendship they'd shared. And his youthful, rash behavior today only confirmed it.

'Twas it her fault if his heart pined for her? Her father granted Riana the right to pick her husband, but what if she waited too long? How long would her father's patience last? Might she end up wed to the young Niall out of necessity?

She tossed and turned in her furs, trying to remedy her lack of affection for Niall with the over-affection she felt for the Roman. *It's because he's new to the tribe, different,* she told herself, like having a new *léine* or bronze torc. And she pitied his status. 'Twas the reason for her interest, at least that was what she told herself. But she was lying, and the gods and goddesses knew it.

Throwing her arm over her eyes, she tried to block out the flickering light of the hearth just as she wanted to block the unbidden sensations that rose in her body whenever the Roman came to her thoughts.

Why did the Roman consume her thoughts so? Her sister and Niall both noticed, and if they decided to share their suspicions with her father . . . well, she didn't want to begin to think on that. Who knew what her father would do? And she didn't want to find out.

Riana sought to harden her emotions against Horatio, view him the same way that the rest of the Caledonii did, but the more she tried to ignore him, to not think about his sun-kissed skin, his rough hands that touched her gently, his full lips. . . Shivers danced across her breasts and to her lower belly. *Stop!* she screamed to herself.

The murmuring noises of the roundhouse had drifted off to rustling and snoring. The sounds of the night were broken only by natterjack toads calling to each other in the fields and loons cawing their lonely songs — the same song her heart thrummed in her pallet of furs. Her body called for a partner to chase the loneliness away, to become one with her, share her life, and though she knew it was wrong, the image of a dark man who spoke broken *Gaelig* came to her mind.

That night, when she slept, she dreamed of Roman heralds and bronze skin.

But she wasn't dreaming alone.

Horatio's sleep was broken, disturbed by his throbbing chest and the image of a red beauty who was beyond his reach. He had missed her company at his evening meal, and anger at Niall burned with the blisters on his skin.

Riana may have been oblivious at how much the blond Caledonii wanted her, but everyone else, including Horatio, could see it plain as the daylight. And that level of unrequited desire was dangerous in young men. Horatio had seen it many a time with his youthful playmates, with his fellow Legionnaires, and with himself years ago. Every man had a story of his youthful love for a woman he'd never have.

He didn't blame the young Caledonii. How could one look upon Riana's stunning comeliness and not be filled with intense yearning? Nightly, Horatio battled his own cockstand at the mere thought of her. And when he let those images run rampant in his mind, envisioning her luscious breasts that swelled against her richly colored tunic-dress, her milky skin that begged for his touch, her red lips that demanded his kisses, he had to use his hand to resolve his hard member and spill his seed into the dirt.

He wanted to spill it into her.

Some days, these lustful thoughts were the only thing that kept him going.

As unrequited as the blond Caledonii's love for the goddess-like Riana may have been, the man had a far greater chance of acquiring the object of his obsession than Horatio did. He was enslaved by this maiden – how could he possibly desire her that way?

A foreign slave with nothing to offer? He had a stronger chance of finding the treasures of Croesus than finding his way into Riana's bed. Or her heart.

So why did he punish himself thusly? Why did he let his thoughts turn to her? But the more troublesome question was, how could he not?

The solution to his desire was plain — he needed to leave. Escape. Before she captured his heart in addition to his body. If he could do that, rejoin his Legion, then perchance this madness would cease. With distance, he might learn if he truly longed for her, and if he did, return as a conquering Roman soldier and ask her to join him.

The other option — of remaining enslaved and pining for her from afar — was not the choice he wanted to make.

Chapter Seven: High Summer Festival

THE SUMMER SOLSTICE grew near, and the villagers busied themselves preparing for the event. As one of the largest celebrations of the year, one that focused its festivities on the bounty and glory of the mother, 'twas also a celebration that demanded much in the way of preparation. And as the eldest daughter of their tribal chieftain, most of that responsibility fell to Riana.

Not that she complained. In fact, she reveled in it. Years of taking on this task had refined her expertise until every aspect was near perfect. As she worked, Riana's skin glowed with a moonlit radiance and her mass of vermilion hair seemed livelier, wilder, in celebration of the mother goddess. 'Twas as if the mother took Riana as her embodiment, where everything red and white and green on earth was exalted.

And her shining visage was not missed by anyone. The villagers expected her reaction to the festival, looked forward to her infectious excitement, and both Niall and Horatio only grew more enthralled with the woman.

Riana noticed none of this. She focused on the Celebration of Alban, and of Rhiannon, the horse goddess of fertility, as part of the feast of *Alban Heruin*. If she exuded any other-worldly aura, she was unaware. Which only made her more bewitching.

Her days were filled with stitching a fine new *léine* for the day of the festival. Some women wore less — a breast covering and a short skirt, a set of bronze or iron links encircling their mid sections. Dressed this way, their red and blue woad tattoos stood out against the fading sun and danced in the firelight. Riana would paint her face and chest in delicate yet complex lines but preferred to wear her *léine* as she worked the festival. It made moving about the villagers and tables of food easier and kept most men's interest at bay.

The rest of her time involved collecting and arranging sticks for the fires and preparing foodstuffs for the feast. So much food – it rivaled their harvest celebration in the fall. She was grateful Tege had recruited her sisters, Maeve and Gwyneth, in addition to several other lassies from their tribal village, to work on the preparations. Boar and venison, a selection of cheese and berries, oats, soups, and if they had a good year, salmon drizzled with honey. And oh, how the mead and ale would flow as the river bubbling from the loch.

Most of the festival took place near the standing stones south of the village. The stones formed an erratic circular shape, and the largest stone was a fingertip taller than the red giant Ru himself. The other boulders reached Riana's head or were shorter

The Maiden of the Storm

— children climbed on them when their preoccupied parents weren't watching.

The stones were a place of reverence and celebration, a place where the fabric of the world wore thin, and the Caledonii came close to the gods and goddesses. And if a young lad or lassie were lucky, perchance a holy vessel might trespass, reaching through the delicate mantle and touch that fortunate soul, blessing them for the year.

It seemed a sound idea, one promoted by the learned *druidai,* but Riana had never felt the touch of the gods. At least, no more than usual in her everyday life. If the fabric of the world was thin near the stones, she didn't notice it. Still, that fact didn't lessen the stones' significance for their tribe.

The men of the village worked on clearing the hillside around the stones for the event and building the pyre at their center for the final evening bonfire. Last year, the fire grew so large that Riana believed the goddess Rhiannon could see the flames from her roundhouse among the stars. The fire, the stones, the sultry air, even if the gods didn't touch her, their power reverberated across the Caledonii lands on the feast of Alban.

Having spent the morning with her sisters, bent over their gowns, squinting as they plied their needles to add fine details of embroidery along the necklines of the *léines* or skirts, Riana needed a break, fresh air, and to stretch her legs. The construction of the pyre called to her, and she set her sewing aside to race out the gate to the hallowed grounds.

Thick, bearded men, dressed only in trews or plaids draped from their waists, lifted tree trunks as wide as their chests, tossing them onto the pyre. 'Twas a vision of strength and majesty, their muscles shifting under their skin and shiny with exertion. Riana paused a moment to enjoy the view. Later that night, these bare-chested warriors would strip down to wear only a swath of plaid around their hips and woad designs on their skin — showcasing their raw power as they danced around the fire.

Niall, his own powerfully broad chest coated in a film of sweat, lifted a hand in her direction. Riana waved back, the excitement of the upcoming event filling her every pore like a heady wine. Niall finished with the lumber he felled, hacked the axe into the tree trunk with a resounding "thwack," and sauntered over to her. His sly grin peeked out of the scruff of his blond beard, shamelessly showing the world he was proud of his strength and how he looked as he worked the trees. Riana returned the smile.

"The preparations are strong this year, Niall," she complemented. Niall bowed his head.

"Aye. 'Twill make last year's fire look like the flames at your hearth!" he joked back. "And the feast? 'Twill rival last year as well?"

Riana's own wry smiled curled against her pale cheek. "We have a few surprises for the celebration this summer," she bragged. "Methinks the tribe will be pleased with the fare."

"As long as Alba is pleased and gifts us with a strong harvest," he responded.

"She will be more than satisfied," Riana assured him.

She turned her head toward his as she spoke, and suddenly found her lips swallowed by his bearded face. Her surprise gave him the time to deepen the kiss, probe her mouth with his tongue before she yanked away.

"Niall! What do ye mean by this?"

"I thought 'twas obvious? We are celebrating the feast of *Alban Heruin*, and with ye here with me, I thought ye wanted . . . " his voice drifted off.

He may have sounded confused, but the gratified look on his face signaled he believed he won something — something

The Maiden of the Storm

that wasn't his to win. Riana flapped her hand at him, waving him away.

"No, 'twasn't. I was here to compliment ye, all the men, on the preparations. I told ye, Niall, ye are nay the one for me. I care for ye, aye, but solely as a friend. Please remember that."

Then, indignant and frustrated, she spun around and marched toward home. The joy of the day had been lost in the lips of a man who wouldn't accept her decision. If he continued to press his claim, she might need to bring her troubles to her father.

Amid these preparations, the last thing she wanted to do was bother him with her petty concerns.

The morning of summer solstice dawned bright and warm, just as it should to celebrate Alba. Fires burned around the village, inside and outside the walls, and at every hearth. Caledonii from other villages arrived to join in the festivities. By the end of the day, boards of rich fare were at the ready. Fresh and dried fish, scorched meats, fruit and cheese, 'twas a feast unlike any other. The air was heady with the sweet scents of food and the smoky essence of the fires. 'Twould be a night to remember.

Eian McLaurin, the celebrated Oak King of the festival, wore a wreath of woven vines and fruit and oak leaves on his head. His face and chest, like most of the tribe, were painted in lines of blue woad and red berry, and a wide iron torc hung around his neck, symbolizing his strength.

And he symbolized it well — as a young man, his shoulders and chest had finally grown into a form befitting a

Caledonii warrior. His legs rivaled tree trunks, robust and powerful. His handsome face framed by dark hair smiled the entire night as he danced with any maiden fortunate enough to turn his eye. More than one lucky lass sought to jump the bonfires with Eian, and their loving helped ensure their tribe's crops might grow lush and plentiful. Rhiannon be praised.

    Riana took a spin with Eian, skipping in a circle with him, her hand raised and pressed against Eian's as they danced. She didn't anticipate jumping any fires with the laddie, though, as her desire did not burn for the earthen-haired Oak King.

    Sweat dripped down her back, wetting the fabric of her new *léine* which clung to her gentle curves in a woad-blue second skin. Many appreciative eyes roved over her exposed shape, fantasies of her wild scarlet tresses, full hips, and lean limbs ensnared a man's lusty thoughts. While most of the young men sagely kept those longings for the chieftain's eldest daughter to themselves, the lads wouldn't be denied. Other nubile maidens were dancing about the fires, including Riana's sisters, more willing young women upon which a zealous man could take a chance, find a mate to jump the flames, and lose himself in between welcoming thighs.

    Niall was not one of those more practical men. His intense gaze followed Riana as she sauntered amid the festivities, watching as she danced with Eian or with her sisters, as she nibbled on a ripe crimson berry that stained her lips as red as her hair, as those lips pulled wide in a laugh. If Niall were to show Riana that she was meant to be his, tonight was the night.

    Finishing off the *quaich* of mead and last bite of roasted boar, he tossed the bone to the ground and marched toward her.

Niall wasn't the only one whose eyes coveted the red maiden. As part of the celebration, servants and slaves were encouraged to attend, serving meat and drink and tending the fires. Though Horatio's hands were free for the event, shackles linked his ankles in a stride's length of chain, much like when he worked in the village. Enough length for him to walk, but nary enough for him to run. Hobbled as he was, Horatio was still able to move easily about the festivities. He even helped himself to the wealth of food, more food than he'd seen in the past several fortnights. And such an array!

If he wasn't careful, he'd make himself sick overindulging.

After claiming another handful of fruit and cheese, Horatio moved to the trunk of a sturdy tree to watch the evening's events. He sunk down to sit at the base of the oak, brushing away a cache of pointy acorns before settling in amongst the exposed roots. His seat under the tree gave him an ideal view of the dancers, including those crazy enough to jump over raging flames —*It explains why they wear almost nothing to this feast. How did they not catch their clothing on fire?* Horatio marveled. Most importantly, he enjoyed a clear view of his personal Celtic goddess, Riana.

Seeing her in her environment outside the hut, her exuberant face and shoulders relaxed, her bosom shining and heaving, was about as close to Elysium that Horatio could imagine. Her blue gown clung and clung, and when she swirled around in a dance, the skirt kicked up, exposing a long length of her milky leg. Horatio fought to keep his groin from showing these barbaric people how excited he was.

He finished the rest of his food and brushed the crumbs from his fingers, his belly rounded and satiated. Gods knew he needed it. The light meals and heavy work burned off every last bit of fat, and his skin pulled taut across his lean muscles that had grown even more sinewy as of late. While he might never reach the mass of these monstrously huge Highlander Celts, he was gaining on them, and was probably the most muscled of his Legionnaires.

The thought of his soldiers left a passing ache in his chest, and a sense of loss and fear that he might not escape and see them again. But he didn't let the dismal notion remain. To do so might well drive him mad. He cast it aside, telling himself that an escape must make itself known to him soon (*it had to, it HAD to,* he promised himself), and his reunion with his men was forthcoming.

'Twas easy to push the sad thought from his mind as he continued to watch Riana. She was a tantalizing distraction. Her face, full of joy, sparkled like the stars as gloaming turned to evening, even more red in the firelight. She was the embodiment of splendor, and both his heart and his cock throbbed as he watched her. He stretched his legs out, trying to find a comfortable position and continue as a voyeur.

The *druidai* gathered his robes and stood at the center of the stone circle facing west as the final thin line of sunset settled in the horizon. The sky became full dark. The *druidai's* importance was symbolized in his position next to Ru, who also stood at the stone center. The chieftain reveled in the night's events, using the festival to showcase his power and his expansive bare chest that dwarfed all other men. Even Tege looked the part of the chieftain's wife, her cool blonde beauty accented with leaves and flowers around her head and waist.

Ru's booming voice commanded all present to quiet for the *druidai's* words. 'Twas the only moment of silence that evening, with nothing more than the popping and snapping of the fires filling the void. Then he lifted his arms skyward and spoke a solemn prayer to the goddess Rhiannon.

Glory of the Day-Star, hail!
Lifter of the Light, Burnisher of the Sky.
Gifts of love to earth are bringing,
Summer's shimmer, dew's delight.
Dancing be the heart within us,
Open be our souls to bliss,
Courage vanquish every shadow,
Greet Midsummer with a kiss.

Riana had finished dancing with a younger lad of her village, one who was still years away from full manhood. Sweat dripped into her eyes from exertion, and her chest heaved with breathless laughter. Even the stoic Dunbraith let down his guard and imbibed and danced around the flames. 'Twas no celebration quite like the summer solstice. When she spun around, an immense hand clasped her arm.

"My turn?" Niall asked in his deep voice scented with ale and spiced mead.

Riana shrugged and smiled, flattening her palm against his and lifting her skirt as they twirled in the glow of one of the smaller bonfires.

Niall's face was at first open and engaging, most likely a result of heady drink, but as they danced, it changed, becoming more intense, more focused. He closed his fingers around Riana's hand and pulled her toward the low bonfire near them.

"Come," he said, his voice thick with desire, "let's jump."

Riana twisted her arm, snatching it from Niall's grip.

"Nay! I told ye, we are no' meant for each other." Riana tried to keep her voice level, kind even, so as not to rile his anger. "Ye are too young and too reckless. Please, find ye another."

"Even as friends, we can share a night of passion. Ye danced with me, smiled at me. I thought ye were encouraging me to ask." His tone rose with aggravation. So much for her kind voice keeping him calm.

She stepped back as he grabbed at her arm again. The heat from the fires met the nervous burning inside her, and a new sweat broke out over her skin. The roaring of the bonfires filled her ears, and the screeching and laughter of the celebrants covered their arguing.

"I've smiled all evening, and danced with many, including Eian. Ye think I will jump the flames with him? Nay. I had no' selected anyone this night, and I would ask ye to respect my wishes." Her fingers pried at his hand, trying to escape from his iron grip. "If no' for me, then for my father!"

Perchance invoking the village chieftain would bring the man to his senses.

"Nay, we are perfect for each other? Why do ye no' see it?"

He continued to yank on her arm, lost in his own frenzy and apparently drunken stupor. His rich flaxen hair stood on end, reflecting the red and gold fires. His hazel eyes mirrored the flames, and he seemed larger in the raging light. And for the first time in her life, she feared him.

"Let me go!"

She hammered at his hand and leaned back, defying his urges with everything she had.

A jingling to her right resonated over the noise of the raucous festivities. A bronzed, muscled arm slipped over her hand and gripped Niall, halting the giant.

"The lady does not want to go with you. I suggest you release her now."

Horatio's firm voice commanded obedience. Riana presumed 'twas his Legionnaire voice, so different from the light-hearted tone he used when they conversed at mealtimes. He was coming to her aid, a surprising action from a slave who could be summarily punished for laying a hand on a member of the tribe. Horatio understood this. Why did he risk such a thing?

Niall puffed up his chest, towering over the Roman by inches. His eyes narrowed to angry slits.

"Watch yourself, Roman slave. Ye overstep. The lady, as ye say, is with me. Come, Riana."

Niall reached for her again, his fingers brushing against her sleeve. Horatio batted it away, blocking Riana from Niall's inebriated advances.

"Horatio, do no' touch him," Riana cautioned, her voice getting lost in the dark chaos of the festival. "Please, 'tis the celebration of Alban!"

In a desperate move, Niall lunged at Riana, only to be met with a fist to his jaw. Stumbling on his heels, Niall shook his head, trying to regain his senses. Riana turned her distraught face to Horatio.

"Go, Horatio. Return to the hut. Now. Please. I dinna think anyone saw ye. Hurry. Ye were never here."

Horatio drew up to his full height, his amber eyes searching hers, sharing a fervid look, a moment that spun out into the night. A loud cheer brought them crashing back down. Horatio forced his gaze from Riana, scanned the crowd to make sure no one was watching, then blended into the shadows back toward his hut.

Recovered, Niall straightened and focused on Riana.

"Where is he?" The confusion in the man's face, either from too much ale or the punch, was unmistakable. Neither was his rage.

"Niall, ye are pissed from drink," Riana reprimanded. "Ye have overstepped. Now 'tis time to find your bed. Alone."

The ferocity of her words was matched by the fury in her hardened face. With her shoulders thrown back and her voice commanding, she was never more Ru's daughter than she was in that moment. An expression of understanding finally dawned on Niall. His eyes widened, and he stumbled into the crowd, losing himself in the throng.

Riana sighed. The man was destined to be someone else's problem this eve, and she sent up a silent prayer to the goddess that he found his bed quickly. She let her gaze rest on the fires, still well ablaze, and at the jubilant celebrants. Her shoulders slumped.

The night, which had begun with such excitement, such delight, had ended so horribly. Niall's misguided actions and her fear for Horatio coming to her defense ruined the great goddess celebration.

Horatio. Her thoughts returned to the handsome Roman again and again.

Lifting her damp locks off the back of her neck in a feeble attempt to cool her heated skin, she wiped her free hand on her skirt and hiked up the hill, eager to find her own bed. Slumber would be a long time coming, but she no longer wanted to celebrate.

Perchance, if any of them slept this eve, they could wake refreshed and forget the ending to this night.

Chapter Eight: Morning After Realizations

MOST OF THE CALEDONII woke with pounding heads and sick stomachs. Remnants of the festival littered the stone circle, and the slaves and servants spent most of their day cleaning up what was left, with several villagers assisting. Clean up was nigh as busy as the daytime preparations, only slower, with added aches that followed a night of drinking.

Horatio, however, woke under a cover of dread. He'd laid his hands on a free man of the tribe. He knew the ways of the world and what happened to enslaved people who rose against their masters. Stories of Spartacus still echoed in the stone-cobbled streets of Rome, but few who enacted violence against their betters met with anything other than death. And even the mighty Spartacus came to an untimely and violent end for his subterfuge. Had Horatio lasted this long as a soldier, then a slave, only to find death's embrace because he defended a woman?

A woman. Horatio had to laugh at his thoughts. Not just any woman. A goddess on earth. Straight from Mount Olympus. Hera herself would have a fit of jealousy over this bold and stunning Caledonii maiden.

Had Niall let her alone afterward? Horatio had hated leaving Riana with the inebriated sot, but he'd had no choice. Riana had commanded he leave, lest his life be forfeit.

And he'd have struck the sot again in a heartbeat.

The village was silent outside the walls of his hut, slow to rise after a night of drunken celebration. This gave him time to consider his options. Mayhap the lass would plead his case, justifying his actions in defense of the chieftain's daughter. Mayhap the man he struck was too drunk to remember how his jaw became bruised.

Either way, Horatio didn't doubt a dire punishment was in his future, should the Caledonii permit him to live. And as he recalled the events of the night before, memories of a dancing, laughing red goddess tinged every memory. As foolish as his emotions may be, that image of Riana never left him.

Even with the threat of retribution and death hanging over him, Horatio knew she was worth the risk.

※

Rolf was standing guard at the hut when Niall approached. He nodded to Rolf, then made his way down the path. His first stop was the bucket of water by the well. His aching head and crusty eyes needed relief before he attempted to approach the day.

The Maiden of the Storm

Dousing himself thoroughly, water dripping from his bare chest to the waistband of his braies, Niall rubbed his hands over his face, trying to chase away the pounding at his temples. He needed the full use of his brain for his next task.

Resting against the well, he waited in the pale morning light, knowing his quarry was to pass by him soon.

He'd barely finished that thought when Riana appeared, stepping from her wheelhouse, looking as clear and fresh as milk. Taking a deep breath, Niall pushed himself off the well wall and approached her on heavy feet.

His shoulders slumped, and he hung his head lower the closer he came to her. Though he recalled little of the night before, he did recall he'd behaved badly, trying to coerce Riana's hand for him, even forcing a kiss upon her unwilling lips. Ashamed at his actions, he woke with a pressing need to apologize and ask her forgiveness.

Niall may have wanted Riana, but he was a better man than how he'd acted at the festival. And he needed Riana to understand that.

"Riana," he called out, his voice drumming in his head with a burst of pain. He cringed, continuing in a low tone. "Please, may I speak with ye?"

Riana paused, her tray held before her like a shield. Niall didn't fault her for her caution – he deserved it.

"Aye, Niall. What is it?" Wary though she was, she kept her voice light, unconcerned. And quiet. From the look of Niall, he wasn't up for handling any loud sounds this morn.

"I must apologize to ye," he said, keeping his mussed blond head bowed. "Ye have made your choice known, and I should no' have overstepped. I have been and always will be your friend and servant. Can ye forgive me and my drunken actions?"

He looked so contrite; Riana couldn't help but forgive him. Everyone made mistakes, and Niall was a big enough man to apologize for his as soon as he sobered. Riana shifted her tray in her grip and placed her hand on Niall's bare arm.

"Of course, I forgive ye, ye lout. Just keep your hands to yourself in the future, aye?"

The smile that crossed Niall's lips tried to reach his eyes but was more of a grimace.

"'Twould seem ye are being punished enough this morn. Is your head badly?"

Niall shrugged with one shoulder, trying not to move his head too much. "As I expected after a night of rich food and flowing drink. 'Tis my punishment for over-imbibing."

Riana clicked her tongue in mock pity. "Weel, Aila is awake. If ye knock at the door, I am sure she will have an herbal for ye to relieve your misery. Run along to her, aye?"

Niall didn't respond, but pivoted on his heel, heading for the roundhouse in a rush. Riana tried to stop the sly grin that tugged at her cheek. The poor man was all but racing for Aila's aid. And he seemed remorseful enough over what had happened the night before. A sudden thought burst into Riana's head.

"Wait!" Riana called out.

Niall halted in his tracks. "Aye?"

Juggling her tray, Riana reached him and again placed a cool hand on his lightly furred arm.

"The word *punishment*. 'Tis a reminder to me. About the Roman —"

'Twas her hope he'd not pursue any recourse against Horatio. Niall's lip twitched, but his stance didn't change.

"What about the Roman?" he asked.

Niall rubbed his jaw at the memory. A bluish shadow tainted his skin under his light beard, a temporary memento of

The Maiden of the Storm

his untoward actions at the festival. Riana tipped her head at the bruise.

"He was only acting in defense of me. He does no' ken ye. He was certain ye only had trespass on your mind — "

With his arms crossed over that thick chest, Niall flicked his eyes at the hut.

"If 'twas why he struck me, mayhap he wasn't in the wrong. My head was muddled with drink and my cock full from the dancing and heat. I canna say I would no' have taken it too far, whether ye were willing or no."

He returned his stark eyes to her face, searching it with an earnest expression. Niall knew he was in the wrong, and that the Roman should not face retribution for his actions. Especially since punishing the Roman was bound to bring to light Niall's transgressions, which the chieftain would not receive well. Niall would indeed be punished more than the Roman over what had transpired the night before.

"I will no' pursue punishment against him. If he can keep my ill behavior betwixt us three, so will I."

'Twas the first logical statement she'd heard from Niall in a while. A flush of relief crossed Riana's features, and she smiled at the giant. Rising on her toes, she gave Niall a chaste kiss on his bruised jaw.

"Thank ye, Niall."

He returned the kiss with a tight smile.

"It doesna mean I have any more respect for the Roman. He's only a slave. But he's a slave with a moral code that protected ye. For that, he deserves a pass."

With a final, painful nod, Niall turned again, retreating to the wheelhouse to find succor with one of Aila's herbals.

Shifting the platter to balance it with both hands, Riana resumed her duties — to feed Horatio and let him know he had challenged fate and won.

Riana and Horatio fell into an easy pattern after the festival. Meals twice a day, complemented with light conversation. The brief time with Riana became the moments Horatio cherished and anticipated the most in his day.

The summer was warm, at least for the Caledonii, many of whom found it humorous to see the Roman continue to wrap himself in a *breacan*, even when 'twasn't raining. One night, just as the sun was setting after a long, bright day, Riana asked him about his strange blanket-wearing proclivities.

"'Tis the height of summer, Horatio," she ventured as she placed his tray at his feet. "Yet, ye still wear full leg braies and wrap yourself as though 'twas winter. Is there something wrong with ye?"

Horatio stared at her as she sunk to the ground in her usual, graceful motion.

"Summer? In this weather? 'Tis more like late fall, early winter for the likes of me."

He pulled the plaid cape more tightly around his shoulders in an exaggerated gesture and dug into the also-familiar boiled meat and dry bread.

"Nay," she said with an air of confident knowledge. "I'm only in my summer *léine*. See? Short sleeves and no wool. What is summer like where ye are from?"

Rarely did she ask about his past life now, fearing that too many memories of home may sadden the Roman, making him pine for a place he'd not visit in this life.

"I don't know if I can explain it. The coasts off the Mediterranean are warm. This weather here? 'Tis like our winters."

"When does it snow?" Utter disbelief tainted her voice.

Horatio chuckled. "In the far north of Greece, it snows in the winter. But in the southern parts, we may only get snow in the mountains. When winter departs, so does the snow and cold."

Her quizzical look didn't leave her face. Horatio had a sudden burst of inspiration.

"The festival!" His countenance lit up bright as a bronze lantern. "With all the fires! Do you remember how hot it was amid the bonfires?"

She nodded.

"That. That is like summer at my home."

"Every day? How do ye do anything in that heat? And sweat?" Her russet brows furrowed, trying to comprehend such a foreign concept. Horatio gestured to her wild mass of wavy locks.

"Well, many women wear their hair up, twining it with leather thongs or scarves. And men cut their hair short. They don't wear an extra cape of hair that you northern Caledonii do here."

"So that is why your hair was short when you arrived!" Her eyes glinted like the forests near the glen. Horatio rubbed his hand over his own overgrowth of hair. 'Twas longer than he'd ever worn it before. He was certain he resembled an unruly hedgehog.

Riana reached her arm across his lap and ran her fingers through his thick locks. Horatio froze. Her body was close enough to his that his senses filled with every part of her — the heady smell of her musk and hair, the sensation of her nails on her scalp, the tickle of her tresses against his cheek. Her breasts, full and peeking above the edge of her thin gown, taunted him, and he found it difficult to breathe.

An animalistic urge erupted under his skin, wanting to drag her to the ground and press his face between that inviting offering, and he fought to keep that urge under control.

Then she sat back on her heels, and Horatio could breathe again.

"Short hair, 'tis nay our way, but if ye wish, I can cut it."

"What?" His body stiffened in surprise.

"Your hair? I have the shears for the sheep. I'm sure we can use a pair on ye."

"You want to shear me like a sheep?"

Her smile widened at his reaction to her offer. She nibbled her bottom lip, assessing him, much like an owl surveying its prey.

"Aye. A bit off the side and back, and ye might resemble a Roman again."

Horatio grabbed the last of his meal off his platter and handed the trencher over to her.

"What do I look like presently?" he asked.

"Ye dinna want to ken," she answered, pulling the tray from his hand as she left.

∽

The next day, Riana found Horatio in the menial job of shoveling peat onto a handcart to bring to the village smith. She held the sheep shears under a fold in her skirt.

"Ye seem to be sweating today," she said as she stepped alongside him.

Horatio stuck the pitchfork into the mound of peat and leaned on it, noting an odd radiance in Riana.

"Ye should have seen me yesterday. I was shoveling manure for the crops."

Riana pinched her nose in an exaggerated gesture. "Aye, that I ken. The whole village could smell ye."

"And that makes it so much the better."

Horatio tossed his head, trying to move the damp locks on his forehead so they didn't drip into his eyes. Riana pointed at his hair.

"Did ye want some help with that?"

Horatio missed her meaning. "Help with what?"

Riana removed the forfex clippers from under her skirt, holding them aloft like a prize.

"I am here to shear ye, like a sheep."

Horatio surveyed her from hair to toe, raising one eyebrow in question.

"Have you sheared anything before? From the looks of your own locks, you've never seen the sharp side of a knife."

Riana tossed her long waves in response. "Do ye want a cut or no?"

Horatio pulled his elbow off the pitchfork, letting it fall with a subtle plop into the peat.

"Where are we doing this?"

He sounded as though 'twas another chore, but in truth, the prospect of a haircut excited him. How did these northern men grow accustomed to so much hair?

Few Caledonii milled about the village — most were in the fields or at labors close to their own roundhouses. Riana gestured to the bench just inside the barn.

"Let's bring this into the light? 'Twould suffice."

Stepping as far as the chains on his ankles permitted, Horatio lifted the edge of the bench and dragged it from the shadows into the sunlight. Riana pressed her hand on his shoulder, encouraging him to sit on the bench. He sat.

Riana's fingers worked through his growth, pinching at grass and other detritus that littered his mahogany locks. The silky strands slipped across her fingertips, and his head fell back at the sheer indulgence of contact with another.

Other than his fist fight with the Caledonii men and a few rare arm touches from Riana and her sister, no one had touched him since his arrival. Not a real touch. A man missed a woman's gentle caress after too long a time, and Riana's tender ministrations on his scalp were more than he could have asked for. Shivers cascaded down his spine. He closed his eyes to enjoy the moment of bliss in full. He didn't want it to end.

A snipping noise sounded in his ear, her fingers moving the shears expertly, nipping at his errant tresses.

"You have a good hand. Seems odd, given few men appear to keep their hair short."

"I canna speak for how 'twill look when I'm finished," Riana admitted, "but 'tis no' too different from snipping the tight areas on a sheep."

"Anything is better than the scratchy hair against my neck."

Too soon, Riana had finished cutting his hair, and she was brushing at his shoulders, flinging the snippets of chestnut locks to fly on the wind. Riana was certain the birds would discover the locks and be fortunate to line their nests with so soft a cushion.

She was wiping the shears against her skirts to clear away any lingering hairs when she felt more than saw Horatio standing right next to her. He'd risen from the bench and waited until her face turned toward his.

He brushed his hands over his head, relishing the sensation of his shorter hair. His face was close to hers, close enough that the heady scent of his manliness from work overwhelmed her senses, the heat of his skin baking her like a fire.

"Thank you for this," he told her, his voice low with gratitude. "The haircut, and your presence, 'twas quite a generous gift."

Riana cleared her throat, trying to tamp down her rising nervousness. Why did his nearness affect her so?

"'Twas the least I could do," she answered, her own voice barely a whisper of breath on his face.

Neither moved; neither left to return to their tasks. The warmth of the sunlight, of their skin, of their shared heat consumed them, drawing them closer, until Riana placed her hand on the defined muscles of his chest, clutching at the spatter of black hairs. Her face upturned, her lips parted in heady breathing.

Horatio didn't know what came over him, but her tempting expression and her palm on his chest were more than he could bear. 'Twas as if that wild animal rose inside him again and took over, wanting to ravage the stunning woman before him.

He settled with ravaging her mouth with his. The dance of their lips grew, becoming more forceful, and when her lips parted more, Horatio touched his tongue to hers in a kiss that demanded everything from her.

His arms slipped around her waist as their kiss deepened, their tongues and lips exploring. His groin pulsed, thickening, and he groaned into her mouth. He was lost and only the distant sound of Caledonii voices brought him crashing back to the barn. Horatio snapped his head away and stepped back in a rush.

"My apologies. I didn't mean —" he tried to speak, but words failed him.

Riana cut her fierce gaze to his face, then dropped her eyes to his chest and lower, before turning slowly and sauntering from the barn. She seemed rather pleased.

If he scared her in his aggressive kiss, she didn't show it.

In fact, if Horatio hadn't known any better, he would think Riana appeared satisfied.

Chapter Nine: Nothing to Regret

HE THOUGHT THAT was the end of it — that Riana would keep her distance from him, treat him as the rest of her tribe did, like an annoying yet useful fly. That the kiss they shared was nothing more than Riana trying something new, a Roman delicacy.

Instead, here she was again with the horses and larger sheep, and Horatio, in the barn. Her sisters had joined her earlier, feeding the animals and leaving before the rain changed from a gentle mist to a full downpour. Her *arasaid* covered her head in a hood, loose wisps of her hair standing in stark contrast to the browns and blues of her plaid.

'Twas no reason for her to return, no reason for her to join him in the barn, no reason for her to tug the barn doors closed. . . . what was she doing? Why had she returned? Had she left something behind?

"Milady, can I help you?"

Horatio stabbed the rough-hewn pitchfork into the stack of hay he'd been tossing into the pens. Dank and heady, the raw animal scents of the barn clung to him in a second skin, and the pattering of rainfall upon the walls and thatched roof filled his ears as he worked. His hair, just as damp as the rest of him, hung limply against his skull as he stood in the middle of the stalls, watching Riana.

His heart thumped in an irregular staccato in his chest when she slipped the bar across the doors, locking them in. Or barring others from entering? The air grew impossibly thicker. His gaze never left her form.

"Milady," he tried again.

This time she whipped around to face him, flipping her hood off her hair. Her deeply russet curls swirled about her head, a red cape shining in the now dim interior of the barn.

"'Call me Riana," she said, her voice husky.

She rushed to Horatio, cupping his jaw between her palms, and kissed his surprised lips. For a moment he didn't respond, his brain in shock. Then all thoughts fled his head, and he wrapped his arms around her in a full embrace, kissing her back with the pent-up passion he'd held in check for so long.

He clutched the fabric at her backside, drawing her in tight against his smooth, naked chest. One of her hands dropped to his rock-hard muscles, where her delicate palm seared his skin.

A slow pressure built under her palm and she shifted, pushing him backward, and he allowed himself to be led to the empty stall at the rear of the barn.

As the play of their lips and hands grew more intense, more demanding, he wondered for a moment if he'd fallen asleep and this was just a dream, a fevered dream from which he didn't want to wake.

She stepped away from him long enough to yank her plaid from her shoulders and unwrap her wide belt so the lengthy swath of fabric fell to the hay, creating a soft bedding. Then she was again in his arms, kissing and licking. Her teeth nibbled at his chest, eliciting a guttural moan he tried to suppress.

She slipped her hand between their bodies, finding his swollen member and squeezing it gently with her nimble fingers through the fabric of his braies. Her caresses made him throb painfully and rise at the command of her hand and the surprise of her touch. No woman had ever been so bold with him.

The hand resting at the base of his neck tugged as she guided him to the hay, laying on her back and spreading her legs under her rucked-up skirt so he could settle between her inviting thighs. The certainty of where these actions were leading hit him like a shock of icy water, and he snapped upward.

"Riana, what are you doing? Surely, you don't want — "

Her hazy eyes studied him as he poised above her. An enticing smile pulled at her luscious mouth, and her fingertips played lightly against his skin, tracing the sharp lines of his face, his full lips, across his neck to those sinewy muscles of molded bronze that flexed under his chest.

A smattering of downy, dark brown hair started at his belly and brindled down to the waistband of his braies, and she let her fingers follow that trail of coarse curls. Horatio sucked in his stomach at the lascivious touch of her fingers.

"I know about ye, Horatio," she whispered. "I've seen ye watch me. Your eyes devour me like a beast with its prey. And I watch ye, the way the sun strikes your hair, making it both dark and light at the same time. The way your strong back works in the fields, and how your words are light and playful, no' dark and angry, when I bring ye your meal."

Her fingers left his skin and tugged on the front laces of her kirtle, letting the fullness of her milky breasts spring forth from their confines below the bronze torc on her neck. Her eyes glazed over with desire, resembling the sky before a storm.

"I see the way ye crave me, Horatio. I canna deny I want ye as well."

∽

The curve of one rosy nipple peeked from the edge of her *léine*. Horatio's eyes were captivated by that shadow of dusky pink, and his resolve left him. Horatio lowered his head to her chest, tugging the nipple past the pale blue hem to find its home between his lips.

Riana sucked in her breath at the touch of his tongue and teeth, arching her back as his mouth plied her skin, licking and sucking. She squirmed and panted as Horatio touched her in every way she yearned to be touched. 'Twas as though he knew what she wanted before she did.

His lips and fingertips were featherlight against her body. She watched his face as he explored her creamy skin, his eyes burning with an intense fire. They were silent, letting their bodies speak for them.

Riana reached for his head, her fingers curling in the cropped hair at the base of his neck. She pulled his face to hers, capturing his full lips, biting at his lower lip. A deep groan sounded from his chest, his soul pouring forth in that groan. His heart pounded like a drum, and the pressure of it echoed against her breasts.

Shifting her hips, she tried to fit the breadth of his thighs between hers. Her skirt caught between them, and Horatio gathered the thin fabric with an eager hand, yanking it to her waist, exposing the welcome opening of her woman's mound.

Impatient with need, Horatio's hand slipped to his braies, uncovering his throbbing member. Keeping his gaze focused on Riana, staring into the turbulent depths of her eyes, he pressed forward in a swift move. His desperation for her effused from him in a thick cloud of desire, and Riana closed her eyes at the sensation of being filled completely.

He made another soul-consuming sound, and found his pace, rocking with her as she raised her hips to meet him over and over.

This. This was what she wanted. Bronze skin met creamy pale, thighs against thighs, a secret interlude of dreams and fantasy away from the real world of status and expectation. This foreign man with sun-kissed skin and hauntingly somber eyes that seized her soul, he was everything her heart, her body, had yearned for.

Their lovemaking rivaled the storm outside. His powerful body owned her, commanded her body and sent her senses spiraling into the nether. Just as her thighs began to quiver with that shaking ecstasy, Horatio clenched above her, grinding as he found his own height and poured his life force into her with a final cry emitted through clamped teeth.

They remained on her plaid, joined as one, slowly letting the sounds of the rain and the village seep into their secluded moment.

Riana wasn't ready to return to that world. They needed to rise, forget this ever happened, and resume their positions in the tribe. Wrapping her arms around the man collapsed atop her, Riana sighed in resignation. Aye, the real world called, and they must part ways.

But for now, they had each other.

The Maiden of the Storm

Horatio rose up slowly, withdrawing from her in an elongated move and adjusting the ties of his braies. He sat on his heels and admired his red goddess — her hair a scarlet pool under a blood moon atop the plaid and hay. Her skirts folded over her hips, giving him a view of the tender skin that led to her sex. The curls there matched the ones on her head, hues of russet and wine, a dark sunset against her thighs.

He ran his fingers through his own shortened locks in a nervous gesture, and he reached out his other hand to help her rise. Riana sat up, brushing her skirts down her legs. Twisting behind her, she lifted the edges of her plaid to wrap it around her shoulders. She picked off a few random stalks of hay, bracing for the walk back home. The rain outside had whipped up to a frenzied storm.

"Riana, I —" Horatio started, but she placed a cool finger on his lips to silence him.

"Dinna say anything." Her quiet voice was a trace of sound in the unmoving air. She remained still, and he stood with her.

They continued to stare into each other's eyes, unwilling to lose that last tenuous grasp of the love they'd just shared. Riana rose on her toes and pressed a quick, final kiss against his lips, then grabbed a basket lying abandoned on the bench and checked the chickens, lifting a few eggs into the basket.

Without a look behind her, Riana jerked the barn door open and, tossing a loose edge of the tartan over her head, hurried into the storm. Horatio's eyes followed her until she disappeared into the gray.

Only then did Horatio move, sagging into the stall door. He needed to be pinched, slapped, any gesture to bring him back to the real world. Otherwise, the moments they had passed in the barn were naught more than a dream to him.

The chieftain's daughter just let him have his way, satiate his need with her in the most intimate act. *Surely, it must have been a dream?* What other reason could the lass have to take him between her legs?

While Horatio resumed his chores, so ordinary a task after such an extraordinary experience, his mind flitted over their interlude, replaying every touch, every sensation that filled his body. His cock threatened to rise again at the mere thought of her.

The questions still troubled him. *Why did she do it?* What reason did she have to lie with him?

For Horatio, his answer was easy — he lay with her because he wanted to, 'twas his heart, 'twas his greatest dream. In truth, he realized he loved her. 'Twas that simple.

But for her – could it be? Horatio almost didn't dare entertain the impossible idea, but it was present nonetheless. Could it be she cared for him, mayhap loved him as well?

～

That night, he wasn't certain if she'd bring his meal or if someone else would have that charge. If she used him for a moment of passion and now regretted it, she might not make an appearance. She might want to sweep the memory of it away, Horatio had no doubt.

And he prayed to his gods that was not the case. His entire being throbbed, desperate to see her again.

Then there she was, in all her wild-haired glory held by a gold band. In his eyes, she seemed to shine more than usual, causing the sun to dim in her shadow. He had to be mistaken — this woman, this daughter of a chieftain, this goddess who put the beauty of every other creature to shame, could never love a lowly man such as himself. Even if he weren't a slave, he was naught more than a soldier, while she was destined for far greater things.

"I wasn't sure if you'd be here tonight," he dared to speak first.

Riana's loose kirtle slid off her shoulder under her damp plaid, giving her a rare, carefree expression. She shrugged that bare shoulder at him.

"Why do ye think such a thing?" she asked as she set his platter on the dirt and sat next to it.

Horatio was reticent, unsure of what to make of her presence in his hut. Or what to make of the coupling they'd shared.

"Well, after this afternoon, if you regretted it, I mean . . . " his voice trailed off as she barked out a laugh.

"What would I have to regret?"

Horatio didn't mirror her lightheartedness. "You don't regret today—?"

She gave him a sidelong glance, keeping her face averted.

"Nay, 'twas my choice, and ye served me well."

His face grew hard at her words.

So, she didn't have a care for him. He was just serving her in a different way, and that knowledge wounded his heart. He felt foolish in having such deep emotions for her, the absurd hope that she may care for him, and he tried to temper any indication that might give his heart away.

"'Tis good then, that I could serve you." His voice was curt.

He picked at his food as she sat before him, her arms crossed atop her knees and her cheek resting on her forearms.

"Do ye? Regret today?"

If he'd tried to swallow any food, he would have choked on it. Surely, he misheard her.

"What?"

"Do ye regret today?" Her eyes were green slits as she assessed him.

"Why do you ask that of me? I thought 'twas obvious? And regardless, even if I regretted it, 'twasn't like I had a choice, given the position I'm in."

The relaxed features on her face dissolved as dew in the morning sun.

"Oh," was the only sound she managed to squeak out, rising in rebuke.

"Nay, not like that," he protested, standing with her as quickly as his chains permitted. Oh, his words were far too harsh, and he despised himself for saying them. Even if she had no interest in him, that didn't stop his desire for her, foolish though it was.

"I ken ye need to be cautious, that ye are biding your time. That at the first opportunity ye will try to escape. Ye think I dinna see how your eyes search the village as ye work? How ye study the wall, the gate, the palisades? How ye measure the Caledonii men and women to learn who is lax in their duties and who is diligent?"

She lifted her eyes to his hooded gaze. His face was hard, as she was saying aloud his deepest, most hidden secret. Or one of them. And he hadn't realized he'd been so obvious.

"Ye are looking for your way out. 'Tis the only thing ye want in the world."

Horatio was stiff, staring at her with a strange gaze. Suddenly his hand, calloused and warm, swallowed her dainty fingers in a gentle grasp.

"You are wrong," he whispered in the dusky light of the hut, motes of dust and thatch peat dancing around his thick chestnut locks.

He pulled her close, as close as she'd been with him in the barn.

"There are two things."

Then he crushed her soft curves to his hard, lean mass, his lips searching her own, caressing her mouth with his tongue.

And she shocked herself by kissing him back. She'd accepted that she had used him for her pleasure, and that he could never see her as anything other than his captor. Yet, here he was, exposing his heart.

Her arms worked without her knowledge, slipping around his neck. The heat of his body pulsed through her gown's thin fabric, and she felt every clenched muscle of his chest and arms. From under his tattered braies, his most ardent muscle throbbed against her hip again, his need obvious and demanding. Nearly as demanding as his kiss.

Horatio shifted, trying to press closer, his need for her tormenting him, raging under his skin, an animal that only Riana could tame.

The jangling of his chains sounded in Riana's ears, and she whipped her face away, reality crashing down on their moment of hopeless fancy.

"Nay." Her whisper carried in an arrow to his heart.

He'd found perfection in this world, found it in her lips, her arms, her thighs, expressed how he felt, and now 'twas being taken away. Conflicted between lunging for her and stepping back out of respect for her station, he sagely chose the latter.

"My apologies, milady. I have overstepped horribly. I pray you forgive my indiscretions."

Riana stood and stared down at him, a green storm raging in her eyes as they roved over his face, his panting chest, his firm hands, and his chained legs. Her hair, escaping from the woven band that failed to keep the locks from clinging to her face, caught little bits of light, teasing him. A dreadful tease.

Without a word, she spun on her toes and ran off, her footprints in the dust the only reminder of their private interlude.

And she was gone — taking Horatio's heart with her.

He fell back onto his pallet. 'Twas then that he knew. He may never have her again, not as he wanted as a lover, a mate, a wife. But he had that one interlude in the barn, a moment of loving he'd cherish for a lifetime. And as long as he stayed in her village, even as a slave, he'd be near her for the rest of his days. And mayhap nights. 'Twas the best he could hope for.

Chapter Ten: A Strategic Plan

MUCH TO HORATIO'S surprise, Riana met him in the barn again a few days later.

The last time they had joined, 'twas fast, heated, with no prelude or anticipation. This time, she came to him slowly, standing behind Horatio as he worked. Pressing her breasts against his back, she dipped her slender hand under his ragged tunic — a gift from Riana for days that were wet or chilled. She wrapped her arms around his waist, letting her fingers caress the lean muscles of his belly, which danced and quivered under her intimate touch.

Another summer storm kicked up outside, the rise in the weather matching the rising passion they shared as her fingers worked their way across his skin as though she owned it. And she did, but in this moment in the barn, she owned him in a different way — in a way he wanted her to own him. She had full command of his body and, the way her hand moved lower, sinking into the plush hairs that led to his manhood, she knew it.

Riana knew what she desired. She craved this man, this stranger who stirred her heart like no other. Lifting his stained tunic over his broad back, she kissed that tanned skin, feeling it pucker against her lips in response. He shivered, unmoving, letting her take the lead and caress him in the ways she wanted.

And even though he wanted to spin around and enter her quickly, she was in charge. So, he remained where he stood, her hands and tongue working over his back and to his chest, sending him into a frenzy unmatched by the crackling and pounding of the storm.

One slender hand slid down his arm, and she grasped his hand, turning him to look at her. Riana touched his face, tracing his cheek, his jaw, his eyebrow in tender caresses that made him quiver. Then she leaned into him, pressing her lips against his where he devoured them like a starving man.

And he was starving. Hungry for her. They both were starving for each other.

The kiss continued, drawing out as their bodies moved closer and closer, their clothing an undesired barrier to what they wanted.

Horatio worked her belt, and it dropped to the dirt as he tugged at her *léine*. Riana lifted her arms, letting him pull it over her head. Fully bare, she stepped away, so he could admire this red goddess. *His* red goddess.

Her hair fell over her shoulders in a waterfall, catching the lights and shadows of the barn in a cacophony of cherries, cinnamon, and bronzes. The contrast of that bright mane against her pale skin made his loins swell. She did a slow spin, and his eyes followed every curve of her body.

The Maiden of the Storm

Once she was finished displaying herself for Horatio, she moved back to him, her hands grabbing the edge of his tunic.

Horatio didn't wait for her. He yanked the tunic over his head and stood stock still, again unmoving. Riana's hand dropped to his braies, loosening the ties, letting them fall to his ankles. In a swift movement, he tugged his braies and foot coverings off, standing in all his naked glory.

Riana touched his chest with a fingertip and sauntered around him, her eyes intense as she took in every hard edge of his body. That fingertip dipped down to his buttocks, following their curve even as he tightened in response, and slipped over his hip to his manhood that pulsed and throbbed.

Her finger followed his smooth length from base to tip and back, and Horatio suppressed a heady groan. Her lingering touches and drawn out play rocked him to his core. He feared he would reach his height into her hand, and he clenched every muscle, forcing himself to remain immobile as she worked her magic.

Just when he thought he'd lose his mind, her hand left his cock and pressed against his chest to have him recline onto the pile of peat behind them.

Horatio lowered himself. His eyes never moved away from hers — he was mesmerized by the storm in her gaze that matched the storm outside. Her eyes held everything from chaos and madness to the promise of joy and release.

Once he was on his back, his staff thrusting upward with need and desire, she lifted herself over his hips and in a swift motion, settled onto his turgid shaft with a gasp and a shiver. Her stormy gaze kept him captive as she slid on his cock over and over, shuddering with each move of her hips.

Horatio grabbed at her outer thighs, his fingers clutching onto her, and he didn't let go. Thunder crashed as she rode him, waves of ecstasy building and building, crashing as the crescendo outside shattered against the world. Only when she threw her head back in her explosion of pleasure did her gaze leave him, finally releasing him, and Horatio didn't hesitate.

One hand moved to her milky breast while the other kept a firm grip on her hip, holding her tight as he slammed his manhood into her smooth, inviting flesh.

The sounds of her panting cries called to him, and he could wait no longer. With a final lift of his hips, he thrust deep inside her as he came, and it seemed his spirit left his body, pulled from him by the maiden who commanded his very life, who owned him body and soul.

This meeting in the barn was an act of raw passion, of two bodies that demanded to be one, of opposite poles colliding.

Riana fell atop his chest, trying to catch her breath. Horatio's warm arms encircled her, holding her to him as though he had a desperate fear of losing her.

And as they both lay there in the dusty barn, they each had the same thought.

The world as they each knew it had shifted and would never be the same.

～

She lay across his naked lap, the black hairs on his leg tickling her breasts and belly while his calloused fingers traced the smooth lines of her back. Her skin felt softer than leather and curved from her shoulders to the globes of her backside in a perfect slope. His leisurely strokes sent shivers racing along her spine and caused her to pucker in goose flesh.

Horatio's joy and contentment exuded from every pore and carried in his voice when he spoke.

"Only in my dreams did I imagine I could have you the first time, let alone a second. You are a gift from the gods."

"Or goddesses," she fairly purred in response.

"Or goddesses," he echoed.

His fingers continued their luxurious swirls on her skin, catching damp tendrils of her hair with his fingertips, and the sensation was enough to cause Riana to melt. She rolled over in his lap to enjoy his touch on her breasts. Horatio's talented fingers danced from her nipples to the shallow swell of her belly and back. A lazy smile was plastered on her face.

"You are a dream come to life, Riana." Horatio was unable to control the torment of love and adoration that filled him. If he didn't tell her, he was sure to burst. "Riana, I — "

Before he finished the words, she sat up in a graceful move and placed her lips on his, silencing him with her kiss.

"Dinna say it," she spoke into his mouth so he inhaled her breath. "We have this now. 'Tis all we have. Ye dinna need to say it."

Her hand fell between them, continuing the promise of her lips. He laid her onto her hay-covered plaid for a second time, loving her slowly and with care as the chains binding his ankles jingled — a reminder of how they were loving each other on borrowed time.

Dark gray clouds and torrents of downpour meant the yard was dim and empty. This time when she left, Horatio followed Riana to the door, and when she opened it to escape into the storm, he grabbed her around her waist, catching her lips in a lingering kiss. Then, flipping her plaid over her head in an attempt to ward off the rain, she raced toward her roundhouse.

Neither of them noticed another set of eyes watching them as Riana left the rain-sodden barn. Those eyes squinted against the rainfall, and once Riana's back was in the distance, the eyes went their own way.

'Twas a struggle for them to pretend as though nothing had happened, that their worlds hadn't collided in an explosion of passion and love. Riana had to force herself not to let her eyes follow Horatio when he was at his labors, and their conversations when she brought him his meals became clipped and awkward. Anything more, and they feared they might expose themselves — Riana was certain Niall tried to eavesdrop whenever she was in the hut.

Riana didn't fret for herself, 'twas nothing to take a lover, even one who was a servant or a slave. But when she was supposed to be searching for a husband? As the chieftain's daughter? To flaunt it before the tribe? Her father's anger was not something she wished to endure.

She worried for Horatio. Many a man in the village would begrudge the slave what they coveted for themselves and take their jealousies out on the Roman. Worse, her father would see Horatio as the perpetrator of a crime, of taking advantage of his daughter, even if she told him differently. That breach was unforgivable, and Horatio's punishment might be a beating, if he was lucky — and if he wasn't lucky?

Ru was no stranger to putting a man to death for a lesser offense. And he didn't care for Horatio as it was.

This enmity wore like a yoke on her shoulders. It kept her awake at night and brought tears to her eyes whenever she let the thought linger.

Their village was a small one, and rumors spread amongst the tribe harsher than the winter wind — hard and fast. Their secret would be uncovered, eventually.

Worse than any of that, the worst of everything, was seeing the man in chains. Her man. Her lover. As much as she tried to harden her heart against him, his flashing eyes and dimpled smile had chipped away at that wall. She'd fallen in love with the Roman, and every day she had to watch the man she loved live in irons.

Getting caught with Horatio might lead to their deaths, but seeing her *leannán* lover enslaved burrowed a cavern of pain in her chest.

And Riana made a silent vow to the Goddess Olwen — she who survived her own thirteen trials for her true love — that she'd not abide his chains, his enslavement, anymore.

She spent the next few days keeping her distance from Horatio, painful as 'twas. When they were together, in the semi-privacy of the hut, guarded half-heartedly by Niall or Eian or another young Caledonii warrior, they kept their words curt. While they endeavored to maintain their light conversation, discussing his labors or meal or banalities of the village, their fingers were busy. With a keen eye on the door, they caressed each other's hands, hair, chests, necks, loving touches hidden from a world that would never understand.

Even they didn't understand. But they didn't care. Horatio ate slowly, lingering with Riana, and she adjusted her *léine* each night before she left, less Niall or some other villager take notice of her clothing in disarray when she departed the hut.

And the entire time, Riana's mind was working. She blew at wisps of hair, clearing them from her face as she tried to work out a plan. She turned over ideas, possibilities, opportunities wherein she could help Horatio escape.

'Twas a dangerous proposition, to be sure. If they were successful, she may never see him again. If he were caught, 'twould mean his immediate death. If she were caught, her sentence might be less — her punishment must still be severe –

perchance she'd even be banished from her home to become a servant in another Caledonii village. But she would yet live.

Could she live, though, if her actions led to Horatio's execution? That prospect hung heavily in her mind, tainting every scenario of escape she ran through her head. The best idea she could construct was one where his absence went unnoticed for the entire night, giving him time to run through the trees to the glen and the Roman encampment by the wall.

Worse, any escape plan meant lifting the key from her father — Ru alone held the key to the chains around Horatio's ankles. Those needed to be removed to make sure his run to the *cnap-starra* was successful. The plan also meant digging a hole in the hut, one not visible from the outside or that could be seen when the guards chained him up at night. Then she had to get that key off the guard.

So many parts, such an audacious plot. Could she accomplish it all? 'Twas impossible, it seemed.

Until she noticed her father remove his keys one night as he stripped off his tunic. He placed the keys in a shallow dish not far from the hearth before he washed himself behind his partition. For the rest of the night, Riana's eyes tracked that dish, waiting for her father to take them back. He didn't.

The keys lay in the dish the entire night.

That was the night Riana's strategy began to form.

The next morning, in addition to a platter of food to break his fast, Riana brought something else, tucked in her belt casually so as to not draw attention.

After she placed the trencher at Horatio's feet, she held a finger to her lips, encouraging him to keep silent. Then she slipped the tool from her belt.

"Why do ye have a pickaxe?" Horatio's eyes screwed up at where she stood. Her hair formed a curtain around them, and she hid the axe behind it. Then she shushed him.

"'Tis a maddock. A wee bit smaller, aye? Something ye can hide if ye can bear to leave your *breacan* behind in the hut when ye work?" she whispered in a hurried tone.

"Aye, I can manage, but why do I need an axe?"

Riana moved her face to Horatio's, pressing her mouth to his ear. "Keep your *breacan* in a pile near the wall here," she explained in a low voice as she pointed to a part of the daub wall, just above the stone foundation. "Ye need to dig a hole, nay too big, and not all the way through the daub. Not right away, anyhow. Not until we are ready."

Horatio blinked rapidly in bewilderment. "Ready for what?"

Her face was blank, void of any expression.

"Why, to escape, of course."

Horatio fell back onto his elbow, but the look on his face wasn't one of horror — it was one of interest. The prospect of escape was always at the forefront of his mind. To hear it spoken aloud? To have someone partner with him in this endeavor? 'Twas real now that it was voiced.

And while he coveted an escape – how could he not? – the pull of Riana on his heart had quelled it considerably. If given the choice, he'd rather be free with her than enslaved and pine for her, but at what cost? What if she were caught? He could never forgive himself if she came to any harm resulting from his escape. Death was preferable to that nightmarish possibility.

Her hand remained extended as these mad thoughts raged in his mind. 'Twas as if time froze as they stared at each other, the mattock dangling between them.

He wanted to be liberated — only if he were a free man did he have any chance of being with Riana the way his heart desired. That final thought made the decision for him.

Horatio grabbed the mattock from her hand.

Slipping his plaid from his shoulders, shivering in the morning chill as he did so, he wrapped the pickaxe in the cloth. His eyes shifted to hers in question.

"Right here," she pointed at the wall. "If ye dig through the wall here, once ye are ready to leave, 'twill be easy to break through the outer daub, and ye will nay be in view of the guard when ye run for the gate. I'll make sure the village gate is unlocked for ye."

Horatio tucked the plaid against the wall as she directed, where it looked as though he tossed it off and left it behind in a pile. Very convincing.

His chains clanked as he sat back in the dirt, and his face flicked to hers, one sable eyebrow raised.

"I have a plan for that. I can get the key to the ankle chains off father. Then I just need to figure out how to lift the key that the guards use to chain ye to the post at night."

Horatio shook his head as she spoke. "'Tis far too dangerous for you. What should happen if they catch you?" He shook his head again with more vehemence. "I will not risk it."

Riana clenched his forearm in a desperate grip and shifted her face so her nose brushed his.

"Ye can and ye will. I canna abide seeing ye here every day, irons binding your ankles, at the mercy of the whims of the tribe. At least if ye escape, ye can be free. I can live with that. But to continue to see ye locked up? 'Tis eating me alive!" Her

The Maiden of the Storm

breath was a hot rush against his face. "Please, please, Horatio. I have to do this for ye. I canna survive otherwise."

His heart raced at her impassioned declaration.

"And what if you are caught?" he asked again. "Your punishment will be dire! You may be whipped at the very least . . ."

She stopped his words with a crushing kiss. When she pulled her face away, tears filled her eyes, making them swirl like the sea during a storm.

"I can handle it. I can take any punishment I may suffer. What I canna endure is seeing ye here. Once you have the hole wide enough, tell me. I will pillage the keys, and ye can leave that night." Her storm-riddled eyes lifted to the sky. "And try to leave when the weather is poorly. The guards will nay look too hard if ye run during a storm."

Riana's full pink lips found his once more, sealing their ploy with a rough kiss before she grabbed the platter from the ground and fled, leaving Horatio alone with his thoughts.

And a maddock.

⁂

The days passed long and trying. Every time Horatio turned his head, he felt that someone saw through him, knew his and Riana's furtive plans. When the guards returned him to his hut, he sweat in the cool summer air, certain that his small pickaxe had been discovered. Was he wrong to think the guards had grown lax in Horatio's complacency? Did they truly believe he'd grown to accept his enslaved status?

It seemed unthinkable that he wasn't discovered.

Horatio had scraped the daub from the wall, spreading the crumbs and dust about the dirt floor of the hut, masking his digging. Only a thin film of daub remained, separating him from the outside world. Again, he marveled that a pile of plaids hid his efforts from the guards. Were they just not looking?

And now that he was so close, with only a fine crust between him and his freedom, he had to wait, bide his time. Riana recommended waiting until the skies opened, yet it hadn't happened. How were they in a dry spell in a country so wet? Horatio's eyes flicked to his escape hole, covered by the plaid. The longer he waited, the more time his guards had to find his subterfuge. 'Twas enough to drive a man crazy.

More than these concerns, though, was his worry of Riana's discovery if she were spotted trying to help him. She hadn't shared her plan to steal not one but two keys. Her role was pivotal and dangerous. What if she were caught? Could he live with himself?

The roll of distant thunder sounded as he dug at a stone embedded in the earth. He lifted his head to the west, watching as late-day gray clouds gathered along the far horizon and a cool breeze tufted his hair.

A storm.

Chills tore through his half-dressed body.

Could he live with himself?

'Twas time to find out.

∽

Riana was gathering beetroot and bramble berries from the plantings near her wheelhouse when the tiny hairs along her face stood upright, then her tresses lifted around her head in a crimson halo. The air shifted, and when the low roll of thunder

The Maiden of the Storm

sounded in her ears, every hair on her body matched the hair on her head, standing on end.

Scanning the grasses as she rose with her basket, she searched for Horatio. She needed to catch his eye, confirm with him that tonight was the night to act. Tonight, she'd make him a free man.

She raced into the wheelhouse where the warmth from the hearth met her like a wall. Her sisters and second mother lifted their faces to her sudden entrance. Riana paused, collecting herself under the attention she drew.

"Storm's coming," she said, covering her peculiar behavior.

"Did ye get all the vegetables, then?" Tege asked.

Riana nodded. "What was ready," she answered, handing the basket to Gwyneth.

"Then come help us here," Tege told her, moving over to make room by the hearth.

Riana put on a casual air as she looked to her father's bedding. No Ru, no key. Not yet.

Ru arrived home not an hour later, soaked to the bone in the rain that rolled in with a vengeance. His russet hair was plastered to his head, dripping from his beard and onto the woven floor mats.

Tege rushed to his side, helping him unwrap his sodden plaid from his shoulders to hang it on the peg by the door.

"Come man." Tege guided him to his curtained bedding.

Riana kept her head lowered but watched Tege undress him from the corner of her eye. Before Tege helped remove his tunic, Ru yanked a wet leather strap over his head, and she heard a clanking sound. The key hitting the bowl near his sleeping platform.

Ducking her head lower, Riana's lips crept across her face in a treacherous smile. Her father was soaked, worn from working, and relaxing at home. Soon after eating, he and Tege would retire, pull the curtain closed, and eventually sleep, and sleep hard. Only hours remained before that key would disappear, and so would Horatio.

Her heart fluttered, a panicked bird of treachery in her chest. Hours.

Chapter Eleven: Liberation

"ARE YE GOING to bring dinner to the Roman?" Aila asked, noting Riana hadn't left for her chore yet.

"Aye. I'm just finishing a few things and hoping the rain abates a wee bit."

"It doesn't sound like 'twill." Aila lifted her moonlit face to the thatched roof, listening.

Riana nodded, taking her time to collect the evening meal for Horatio.

"Ye are right. Now or later, it does no' matter," she answered, but didn't hasten her pace. She hoped her sister departed and that her father was asleep enough to grab his key.

Aila stopped listening and returned her attention to Riana. "Weel, dinna wait too long. Ye dinna want to starve the lad. He's naught but skin and bones as 'tis." Aila lifted the cloth she was working on and moved toward her sleeping pallet. "Good eve to ye, sister."

"Good eve, Aila," Riana responded, not looking up.

The wheelhouse fell into a lull of sleepy quiet. Steady breathing, low snoring, and Riana focused herself to remain calm. No need to rush, no need to disturb anyone.

Once the platter was full, complete with some extra vittles in case Horatio needed it for his travels back to his Legion, Riana set it near the door. She seized her plaid, throwing it over her head and shoulders. Then, on the lightest toes she could manage, she stepped to the flax curtain behind which her father slept with Tege. With a nimble touch, she lifted the key soundlessly from the bowl and palmed it, then grabbed the platter and worked her way outside into the rain.

Only then did she release the breath she'd been holding. Now for the second part of her ploy. This one was, if possible, more difficult.

Niall stood near the overhang of the door, his face hidden by the hood of his *breacan*. He peeked his eyes from under the wool and brightened when he saw Riana. She placed the platter on the ground under the wide ledge, her father's key hidden under the bread.

But the key that chained Horatio to the inside of the hut was tucked into Niall's sporran — a loose swath of leather that hung from his waist.

Conflicted thoughts warred within Riana. A dense weight of guilt sat as a stone in her chest. She was making Niall a part of this escape, forcing culpability upon him without his consent, or even his knowledge. And she was playing on his emotions which she had already tossed aside so callously. Nevertheless, it needed to be done.

The Maiden of the Storm

Riana moved close to Niall, tugging on his hood in a tease. She flashed a smile at him, her face near enough to his cheek to graze him with her lips, which she did.

"Are ye staying dry this eve, Niall?" she asked, letting her hands slide over his tunic-clad chest, darting to his braies.

He sucked in his stomach at her provocative touch, and his own lips brushed against hers.

"'Tis a wet night. Company is most welcome," he whispered against her lips, not questioning why she was suddenly kissing him after months of denying his advances. He was an over-eager young man. He welcomed any affections she offered.

And Riana knew this and used it against him. While one hand fondled his burgeoning member under his braies, the other fiddled with his sporran, easily finding the key and lifting it from his person.

"What is all this?" he asked as he encircled her with his thick arm.

"No man should be stuck in the rain so. Ye should find your hearth soon. I dinna want ye to catch ill. Consider this my appreciation."

She gave his cock one more squeeze and his lips one more kiss. Then she patted his chest.

"'Tis for ye, Niall. Something to keep ye warm until your sentry shift is done."

Flashing him another smile, she crouched to retrieve the platter and left Niall to his fantasies in the rain.

The Maiden of the Storm

Horatio's dusky head lifted from his arms when Riana entered in a flurry. Instead of his typical relaxed expression, his face was tight, anxious.

"I have everything," she said in a rush, placing the trencher on the ground. She held out Niall's key. "Here is the key to the chains that bind ye to the wall of the hut. Leave it behind when ye depart. Perchance someone will think they dropped it for ye to find."

'Twas a paltry attempt to protect Niall, but 'twas the best she could offer the poor lad. She leaned over the platter and raised the bread, exposing another bronze key.

"This is for the chains on your feet. I dinna care what ye do with this key."

Whether 'twas found or not, her father would know regardless. She didn't say as much to Horatio, who would never go along with the escape if he understood how quickly she'd be accused. But she knew.

The moment he woke and tried to retrieve his key, Ru would realize who committed this vile crime, his retribution immediate and severe, without question.

But any punishment was worth it. Seeing Horatio's bronze face eager and full of hope set her resolve. 'Twas one gift she could give him. The gift of his freedom.

"Extra food, too, for ye. Niall may leave soon, once he thinks ye asleep. I encouraged him to do so. Wait a bit, undo the chains, break the rest of the wall, and run. Promise me. Ye will flee like your life depends on it, because it does. Run and do no' look back."

She grabbed the platter and stood in a rush. Horatio scrambled to his feet with her and took her hand.

"Thank you, Riana." He didn't know what else to say to thank her.

She was doing too much, taking on too much risk. He gathered her in his arms and kissed her with every ounce of passion he held inside. Their lips and tongue danced, and he lost himself in her before she pushed him away.

"I must go. Remember, Horatio. Run, and do no' look back."

Her last command would be the most difficult. But he nodded in acknowledgment. Riana spun and was gone in a flash of red.

Horatio's heart pumped in his chest, desperate to follow her. That final command — don't look back. He had to force himself to obey.

Because his heart didn't want to.

⁓

Niall caught her arm as she exited the diminutive hut, whirling her into a full hug, jostling the platter which fell to the mud.

"Ye can join me in bed, milady," he spoke in a husky tone, "if ye want me to be warm this night."

His lips skimmed across her jaw as she pushed him away with a gentle hand. She'd expected this reaction, that he would take her earlier kiss and caresses as invitation. Riana had to play coy. The last thing she wanted to do was to anger him or cause him to question her motives.

"Nay this night, Niall." Her voice was stern, but she kept her smile light. "Your shift for the night is done. Mayhap if I feel the need later, I shall search ye out."

'Twas a false promise, one that played on his feelings toward her, but she needed him to believe her. To leave his post and find his rest early. And to do that without her. Riana may have toyed with his emotions, but she wasn't about to take it to his bed.

Fortunately, he accepted her rebuke with a pleasant manner and hope in his eyes. She gathered the platter from the mud and, pulling her *arasaid* over her head, raced into the storm toward home.

The roundhouse was quiet, only the sounds of sleep, the fall of rain, and the remnants of the fire filling her ears. She'd rinsed the trencher before entering and set it aside with the kitchen goods. Everything from dinner, sewing, and weaving had been put up for the night, and Ru's daughters were abed.

She hung her dripping plaid on her peg and slipped out of her sodden *léine* to don her dry shift for bed. The welcome warmth of the roundhouse chased away the chill from the rain. Twisting her damp hair up with a heavy iron pin, Riana slid under her plaids and furs that enveloped her in more warmth.

But 'twasn't enough to stop the chills that wracked her body. Even her teeth chattered, and Bronwyn must have heard her. Her dark head peeked around the bed curtain.

"Are ye well, Riana? Ye sound ill."

"I am fine, Bronwyn. Just a chill from the rain. 'Tis a cold one. Go ye to sleep."

Her sister's black eyes blinked at her, then she crept back behind the curtain. Riana listened to the rustling of Bronwyn's bedding before the lass calmed and, Riana supposed, fell asleep.

That same ending didn't happen for Riana — she tossed under her coverings. She tried to forget the events of the night, tried to forget that she'd played on poor Niall's feelings for her, lied to her family, betrayed her tribe, and put Horatio's life in danger if he was caught in his escape. So much could go wrong. And in the morning, when she must enter the hut and discover him missing — how long would it be before Niall reported she was the last to see the Roman? Before her father made sense of all the pieces, including his stolen key, and questioned her involvement?

Her father was not a stupid man. He'd figure it out sooner rather than later.

The night ticked by at a plodding pace with the rain pattering against the thatch. And sleep never came.

⁂

The next morning bloomed slowly, the rain no longer a violent storm but a gentle, lulling patter of droplets. A cleansing rain. A welcome rain.

But for Riana, an accusing rain. One that she hoped washed away Horatio's tracks and footprints.

Rising from bed, Riana wrapped her tartan coverlet around her shoulders to fend off any lingering chill from the night and set to completing her morning chores. She started by stoking the fire at the hearth and setting the pot of oats to boil. Moving about as quietly as possible, she finished her tasks and then sat on her bed pallet, sewing absently, trying to pretend everything was as it should be. Trying to keep busy.

The rest of her sisters rose with languid idleness. *Oh, the peace of a clear conscience,* Riana chastised herself. Before her father woke, however, she scooped a handful of the oats into a wooden bowl and added a hunk of bread to the platter. She wanted to be far away from the roundhouse before her father noticed the missing key.

Grabbing her still damp *arasaid,* she covered herself and the platter and headed into the rain, ready to play her role. At least she hoped to play this role. 'Twould not do to have missed out on a night of sleep and risk the missing key for Horatio to still be in the hut.

Gavin stood at the door. *Least 'tis nay Niall,* she told herself. Nodding to the hale young man, she pushed in the door and paused.

An iron key lay next to a pile of chain. Horatio was gone.

Riana waited a moment to collect herself, then put on her guise of ignorance and popped back out the door to Gavin.

"Where is he?" she asked.

Gavin cut his sleepy, morning-guard duty eyes at her.

"What do ye mean? He's right there in the hut."

"Nay, he's no' here. Did ye take him out to work before his morning meal?"

Gavin turned to face her, then flicked his gaze to the door before bursting into the hut.

The empty hut.

"What—?" Gavin breathed, searching the narrow space.

With only a post at the rear, there was no place to hide. Riana followed him in, still holding the platter like a shield before her.

Gavin moved to the rear of the hut where pale light cast its rays through a jagged hole in the daub wall. Crouched low, he pressed a disbelieving hand to the hole, and then grabbed at something glinting silver on the ground. The maddock. Riana held her breath, shaking under her skirts.

He uttered a low-voiced curse, *mhac na galla,* then stood in a huff.

"Riana, get ye back home. Tell Ru I have need of him here."

"But what —"

"Now, Riana!"

Unaccustomed to being commanded but knowing she needed to keep up her guise, she raced from the hut, food spilling awry, calling for her father. 'Twas only a matter of time before they guessed her complicity, but she extended it for as long as she could, if for no other reason than to help Horatio run as far from the Caledonii as possible.

Tege met her at the wheelhouse entry. "What ails ye, Riana? Why do ye scream like the sons of Balor are after ye?"

Riana pushed past Tege, flinging the platter to the side. "Is father here?"

"Aye, he's still abed —"

Riana rushed to her father's bedding and flung his curtain aside. The man snored in blissful oblivion. She took a moment to commit his peaceful face to memory — she doubted his face would ever again be this peaceful when he gazed upon her.

"Father!" Riana shook his thick body as she cried to him.

The immense man peeled open one eye from under his bushy brow.

"Riana, please, ye behave as a child. Why do ye disturb a man's sleep?"

He made to roll over and ignore her when she spoke again.

"'Tis the Roman. He's gone."

Ru moved effortlessly for a man so large, and he was upright in bed and wide eyed before Riana took another breath. His expression was no longer peaceful, his bright green eyes clawing at her face like an osprey's talons. Riana shuddered.

"Speak again," his harsh voice demanded.

"He's gone. 'Tis a hole in the wall of the hut —"

Her words broke off when he leapt from his bed, drawing his plaid around his naked waist.

"Who's the guard?"

"Well, this morn 'tis Gavin —"

"And last night?" Ru growled as he yanked on his braies and footwear.

"Niall. 'Twas raining."

"Bring Niall to me. I'll be at the hut with Gavin. Have Niall bring his father and Dunbraith with him. Tell no one else."

He moved to grab his leather thong that housed his keys, including the key to the Roman's chains. So much for being gone in this harrowing moment. His body froze in shocked awareness that the strap was missing. Looking directly at Riana, his face tightened as she cast her gaze askance. He said nothing and withdrew his empty hand from the bowl.

And with that, a bare-chested Ru took three long strides and was out the door into the misty rain.

The prospect of being a messenger for Niall filled Riana with dread. She'd planned to return home and remain with her sisters for the rest of the day. Interacting with the man she had set up as part of her subterfuge? That was a thought she'd not entertained.

But now that the moment was here, and Horatio was gone, what had they missed? So much — too much. Her role in all this was sure to be discovered even sooner than she'd anticipated, given Ru's expression when he found the key gone. She dragged her feet to Niall's roundhouse at the edge of the village, a pathetic attempt to delay the inevitable.

Her lustrous hair sprung up in chaotic waves in the rain, and she undoubtedly looked a fright when Niall's buxom mother responded to her pounding at the door.

"What brings ye here, lassie?" Niall's mother asked.

"My father wants to see Niall at the slave hut."

The woman's eyes widened briefly, then she regained her composure.

"Why's my lad needed there so early? He's still asleep."

"I canna tell ye why. My father says to have Niall bring his father and Dunbraith with him when he comes."

Riana couldn't face the unwitting woman any longer and spun on her heel back toward home.

Though she had hoped to spend the rest of the day weaving by the heat of the hearth, feigning innocence, the shivers that coursed through her body wouldn't be settled by any fire.

Chapter Twelve: Betrayal and Punishment

AFTER THEIR INITIAL meeting, Ru's men gathered swiftly, and she heard them ride for the main village gate. Once she was confident they were no longer in the village, she excused herself, claiming a need to check on the horses and sheep in the village barn. Tege said nothing as she left, not even lifting her head at Riana in acknowledgement. Aila and her sisters, though, watched Riana, their faces perplexed masks of fear and concern.

Riana needed the break. She yearned for fresh air and the nonjudgmental, fret-less contentment of the animals. The air at home was thick, suffocating, but here in the large barn, cool breezes pushed past the cracks in the stone and daub walls, and the refreshing rain washed everything clean. Everything but her conscience.

The soft beasts welcomed her, touching their noses to her hands in hopes of pats and pets and treats. Their gentle sounds lulled her into a much-needed sense of complacency, false though it may have been.

And as she tried to find a moment of peace in this quiet place, she sent up wishes and prayers that 'twas not all for naught, that Horatio made it far beyond the grasp of her father and the Caledonii tribe.

She didn't know how much later 'twas when the barn door creaked, and a fearsome shadow filled the entire space in the doorway. Riana didn't want to believe that she was hiding, cowering from discovery, but in truth, 'twas exactly what she was doing. She remained seated in the far recesses of the barn, a tiny lamb on her lap.

"Riana, are ye there?" Niall's voice called.

Discovery was inevitable. She stood, setting the lamb back in its pen with its mam.

"Aye, Niall. I'm here."

"Gavin is outside. Ye are to come with me."

"My father —?" she began as she approached the familiar shape.

"Dinna say a word, Riana. Just come with me, please."

Only when she reached his side did she comprehend the horror of her actions. His face was a bloody mess, and instead of standing tall and powerful, he hunched over — presumably to cushion injuries on his belly, perchance even a broken rib or two. Dunbraith had enjoyed his task of beating the man who failed in his guard duty.

Her heart clenched at his mass of cuts and bruises, and as she reached her fingers up to touch his face, he grabbed it with a hard hand.

"Dinna touch me."

The Maiden of the Storm

Any care Niall had felt for her had been beaten out of him before he came to the barn.

The distress that wore on her like a cloak for most of the day surged into a panic over her own wellbeing. Niall's injuries were significant, harsher than she'd expected for the lad. Nothing like this. While she'd known she would be punished for her actions, surely she'd not be put to death?

Niall yanked her outside where Gavin, his face matching Niall's in a bruised mess, gripped her other wrist, grinding her bones together. Their rage, though understandable, was also plentiful. Niall's voice tried to temper his fury, but Gavin's emanated from his body like a flame.

Niall and Gavin dragged her before Ru, who sat stiff-backed on a wooden chair near the hearth. His bored expression didn't hide his anger — it suppurated under his skin in a fever. His face blistered red with it.

The roundhouse seemed to narrow as they threw her at her father's feet. He tossed a few handfuls of peat into the fire, letting the heat of the fire add to the heat of his fury. Riana quivered in his presence. He had figured it all out so soon.

She noted the tattered plaid that he held in his hand — Horatio's *breacan*. He had abandoned it to hide his tracks. No plaid meant no threads caught on tree branches to reveal his path. Riana briefly wondered how he managed to cover his footprints in the mud.

"Ye helped him escape? Ye set the Roman free?" Ru's voice was a harsh whisper in the dusky air. "I trusted ye, Riana. Why have ye done such a thing?"

She bit at her lip. A lie must suffice, because she couldn't tell him the truth. Assisting in the liberation of a slave was a vile act. To admit she had lain with him? Cared for the man? Livid wasn't a dark enough word to convey her father's emotions. She hung her head and didn't answer, hoping his anger might burn itself out as he reprimanded her.

Instead, her father leaned forward on the chair, pressing his face close to his daughter's.

"Do ye ken what ye have done? Do ye admit to setting the Roman free?"

"Father, we have never seen eye to eye regarding the Roman," Riana began, evading the question.

Ru stood in a rush and threw his chair across the length of the house, where it smashed into the wall on the other side. Riana and her guards jumped at his burst of anger.

"Dinna try to talk around this, Riana! What have ye done? In addition to setting the Roman free, where he can now return to his troops and bring them here to rain disaster upon us, ye did something worse. Do ye ken that?"

Riana shook her pale, fearful head. While she hadn't considered that aspect when making her plans for Horatio, she also believed in her deepest heart that he wouldn't betray her like that. 'Twas then that Dunbraith stepped from the shadows of her father, his face a glowering mask of rage.

"Ye disobeyed a direct command from your chieftain," Dunbraith growled, his voice dropping low. "Ye betrayed your tribe, your people. Do ye ken the punishment for that?"

Honestly, she didn't. She'd never seen anyone contradict her father before. Riana kept her gaze downcast as he glowered above her, her hair hung in dank strings before her eyes. Her skin was mottled and sweaty from the heat and her circumstance. Worst of all, her brain seemed frozen, unable to form a single thought.

The Maiden of the Storm

Though the missing key might have been enough to convince her father, to be found out so soon? Something else had to have happened. Something she didn't consider. One stream of questions kept resurfacing in her mind: did someone see her with the Roman? How much did they see?

Riana had foolishly believed she had hidden everything so well. Who had known?

The silence drew out, and even in the heat, Riana shivered, pulling her *arasaid* tightly around her shoulders, an armor against her father's attack. What weak armor 'twas.

"Death, 'tis the worst punishment." Dunbraith's voice echoed in the confines of the wheelhouse.

All the air was sucked out of the room, and Riana dropped her head impossibly lower.

"But 'tis your first offense," Ru interjected, "and ye have served me well as a daughter until now, so I think death is too harsh a punishment. And 'tis nay like ye took the life of a kinsman. He's only a Roman."

She wanted to let loose a sigh of relief that Ru's words meant a lesser retribution. Yet, a dire punishment nevertheless hovered in her future. Her father was still chieftain, after all. And she *had* betrayed him. She tried to find some answers to her questions, to plead her case.

"Father, how do ye ken 'twas me? Who told ye?"

"'Tis of no concern —" he began.

"Nay, 'tis my concern whom I can trust! Ye, father, I well understand your position and need to punish me, but who else?"

The desperation in her cry rose to a fevered pitch as she sat up on her heels, sweeping her gaze about the room.

"Ye, Niall? Have ye been spying on me?" She shifted her eyes to Gavin. "Ye, Gavin?"

"Riana! Silence!" Ru's voice boomed. "If anyone did report ye, they did it out of fealty to their chieftain! Just as I expected ye to report any treasonous behaviors to me!"

"I should be able to know my accuser! Which of ye men is trying to get on my father's good side, thinking to bring his daughter low —"

"'Twas me," a light voice called from the shadows. The guards stepped to the curtain as Riana turned to face the voice.

"Aila?" Riana's voice was barely audible in the room. Her breath rushed from her chest and her head swam. "Aila?"

Her sister stepped into the circle of light cast by the fire. Her loose hair, so similar to Riana's, caught the light and shades of wine and cinnamon danced around her head. Aila's eyes were red-rimmed and haunted, the green washed out into a pasty scowl.

"I saw ye," Aila told her. She then squinted her eyes, conveying hidden meaning to Riana that she apparently didn't tell their father. "I saw ye."

Riana clutched at her chest. Betrayed by her own sister? And if she saw what she was suggesting without informing their father as much, how could Aila do this to her? Aila was her oldest, dearest friend and confidant. She had cared for Riana's cuts and bruises while Riana sheltered her from the rough edges of the world. Aila was not only her sister, but the sister of her heart. Of the events of the day, this surely was the worst to bear.

"I feared for ye, for us," Aila implored. "Father needed to know that ye stole the key to the man's shackles. I saw ye take it from father's bowl."

There, she confirmed it. Aila hadn't told their father about Riana's secret relationship with Horatio, and her weepy eyes communicated that she was sorry for even having to share what she did with Ru.

Riana wanted to hate her — the emotion settled deep in her bones — but Aila was just being a dutiful daughter. Something Riana hadn't been. How had Aila's behavior been any different than what Riana had condemned Niall to? Her father had the right of it. Riana had betrayed everyone for her heart. How had she been so thoughtless? Could she have tried to speak to her father about Horatio? Why hadn't she done that before acting so rashly?

"Ye shall be flogged," Ru told her. "Four lashes should suffice, administered by Niall. Then ye shall ride with us when we set out to retrieve the lad. We canna let him return to his soldiers."

"NAY!" Riana sprung to her feet at her father and was held back by Niall and Dunbraith.

Had she done all this for nothing? Only to have Horatio returned to his imprisonment? And then to have the man she betrayed with her actions administer her beating? 'Twas mad! Ru cut darkly suspicious eyes at her before departing the house.

Aila raced to where Riana struggled against the powerful arms of her captors. Her thin arms wrapped around her sister.

"I'm so sorry, Riana," she whispered into Riana's ear. "'Twas dangerous, what ye were doing. I thought this best."

Riana's heart broke at the sad words of her sister. She wished she could forgive her but was not able to in this moment, with her arms held behind her, awaiting a beating and then the eventual capture of her lover.

She pursed her lips in silence as Aila slipped back to the shadows. The men dragged Riana from the house to the post outside the bailey.

"And what of ye, Niall?" she hissed at the staunch young man, lashing out in her anger and shame. "Ye were supposed to guard the hut. How did he get past ye?"

"I have already taken my beating for my part in this, this atrocity ye dragged me into. But while mine was just a lapse in duty, I didna betray our chieftain or our tribe. Even now, I am showing my chieftain just how dutiful I truly am."

Niall knotted the leather around her wrists and then looped it over the hook on the post. 'Twas a bit too tall for Riana, who had to extend on her toes where she stood. Her eyes swept around her wildly. Very few kinsmen were present to witness her humiliation — and those in attendance were the same who happened to be in the yard when she was brought out, and they scuttled away. They did not want to be a part of this display, and she was thankful for the lack of audience.

"I dinna ken why ye did what ye did," Niall said in a low voice so Gavin wouldn't hear. "I have always cared for ye. Ye have a gentle heart, and I know slavery doesna sit well with ye. I will try to be light in the lashing. Your father has asked to keep this private, so ye will no' stay in the public eye. Dunbraith wanted a more dire punishment. Be grateful. We ride out shortly after this."

The prospect of riding on a horse after a lashing made the whole punishment even worse. She tried to tamp down the panic rising in her chest. As with any harrowing event, she needed to focus and breathe if she were to undergo such a beating.

A ripping sound echoed as Gavin tore at her *léine*, rending it to expose her creamy, unmarked backside.

"Such a pity," Gavin commented before stepping back.

Niall leaned into her once more. "My apologies, lass."

At least he didn't hate her enough to regret the action he needed to take. The lash hissed in the air before landing across her back with a crack. The sensation rocked her on her toes, the burning pain immediate and consuming. And this was a light hand?

Three more lashes in rapid succession followed, each with its own piercing burn, then 'twas over, and Niall was winding the lash as Gavin tugged her *léine* back over her shoulder and released her hands. He caught her as she stumbled, and Niall took her other arm as they walked her back to the roundhouse.

"I know ye will no' like it, but ye must let Aila put a poultice on the wounds," Niall told her in that same low voice. As though they shared a conspiracy. "Ye will have need of it afore we depart. 'Twill dull the pain and help heal the wounds."

He paused at the door of the house, holding Riana's shaking form upright.

"Again, my apologies, Riana. I may have detested the man, but I didn't want for it to end this way for your Roman."

Riana must apologize to Niall eventually, but the words wouldn't come to her lips. Niall's haunting speech echoed in her ears as they returned her to her family, laying her gently on her pallet out of sight of her father.

~

Ru had departed right after she'd been returned, no looking back at Riana at all. Aila stood to the side of the house, again hiding in the shadows when Riana came back. Once the men exited, she moved forward, her hair now pulled back in a braid and her bowl of soothing poultices clutched against her chest.

Riana knew what it took for her sister to become involved. She didn't know exactly what Aila had seen, but she knew Aila wasn't fond of conflict. Aila believed herself above that, too pure for the lowly machinations of man, too focused on her healing arts. To come forward to her father, admit what she'd seen Riana do, must have taxed her conscience.

And it must have meant that she was deeply concerned for Riana and her actions. She said as much by way of apology.

"Riana," Aila's voice was a wisp of air in the wheelhouse, "I hope ye can understand why I told father. I did no' think it would go this far . . ." Her voice drifted off.

Riana didn't answer. Her own feelings were conflicted. Anger at her sister burned within her, the sense of her sister's betrayal ran deep. But Aila was her sister who loved her and at her heart, a healer — her only aspiration was to prevent or heal injury. If she believed Riana to be in danger, then of course the lass would report any strange goings-on to their father.

This tension helped keep her mind from her scorchingly pained backside as she lay on the pallet. Aila's treatments, though necessary, were both cooling and aggravating to the lash wounds. The sensation of the thin flaxen cloth was almost too much, but Aila's healing salves were magical, and after a short while, Riana's wounds were manageable.

"I did no' mean to bring harm to ye," Aila told her as she lay the strips in layers across her back. "I'd seen ye with the Roman, and I'd seen the way the Roman looked at ye. I had the sense that something might go awry with the lad. He used ye horribly —"

"He did no' use me, Aila," Riana said with ragged breath. "I chose to help him escape."

"But he convinced ye, to be sure. He made ye promises?" Aila's light fingertips had paused, waiting for Riana's response.

"Nay," Riana answered in a flat voice. "'Twas my choice. 'Twas my idea. He did no' want to leave and put me in danger. I persuaded him otherwise."

The Maiden of the Storm

Aila crept around to the front of Riana's bedding to stare her sister in the eyes. Aila's own face was pale and skeptical. She didn't believe Riana.

"But why did ye do such a thing? Are ye so against slavery? Ye've nay done such a thing afore!"

When Riana dropped her eyes, Aila let a gasp escape. Unlike Riana, Aila lacked any guile.

"Did ye care for the man? On my life, Riana! What were ye thinking? 'Twas foolish by half."

Riana's dull eyes narrowed at her sister, who spoke a harsh truth she didn't want to hear.

"I dinna ken, Aila. But my chest ached whenever I saw him in chains, and when we were together, I felt like my heart soared. Perchance 'twas a reason the Great Mother brought him to me. I dinna care. I love the man, and I shall nay live in freedom while he was in chains. 'Tis all I can say."

Aila gaped at her sister, studying her with mystified incredulity.

They'd been raised as one, it often seemed to Aila, as they were so close in births. And though they resembled one another so much their father oft confused them when they were children, two sisters could nay be more different. Riana was always in their father's sights, the second in command son he'd never had. Aila, conversely, lived in a separate world, keeping to herself and her herbs. Yet, when life was overwhelming or Aila needed an ally, Riana was there without question.

That dedication only increased Aila's guilt over reporting her sister's actions, and she pushed a lock of russet hair from her face in frustration. Every option seemed a poor one. What mattered was Riana, and if the Roman wasn't taking advantage, seeking to ruin Riana, if her sister loved the man, then perchance Aila had been in the wrong.

The heart was more powerful than even a healer like Aila could comprehend. Who knew what drove people to do what they did when the heart demanded? When love called like a banshee on the wind?

Aila shook her head, trying to clear the thoughts that plagued her as she watched her beloved sister cringe under the weight of her lashes and dressings. The wounds would heal — Aila had used a light hand and her best poultices to make sure scarring was minimized — but would Riana's heart heal having been betrayed by her sister and losing the man she loved, all in one day? Or would it remain scarred, matching her poor backside?

"I am so sorry, sister," Aila whispered into the heady air. "I did no' ken your reasoning. I should have spoken to ye afore I acted."

Riana reached out a trembling hand and rested it on her contrite sister's thin arm.

"I ken ye, Aila. Ye did only what ye thought best, to protect me, our kin, and our clan. I shall never blame ye for what happens from that. 'Twas my choice, and I behaved knowing the consequences. Ye are nay to blame for any of this."

Aila hung her head as she listened. There was blame enough for them all. Her wild locks had come loose from her braid and draped limply in her face, hiding her eyes. She daren't look at Riana for fear that she'd never stop the tears once they fell. And if she caught Riana's forgiving gaze, fall they may.

Niall had the horses at the ready near the village port gate. With a gentle hand, he helped Riana atop the impatient horse that pawed at the mud, anxious to be off after too many days cooped up in the stables.

Swinging up behind her, Niall made sure to keep a space between them so as not to touch her abused back. Riana made a silent vow to apologize to Niall once this night rectified itself.

She kept her head low as she sat before him, not looking at anything other than her hands on the saddle. Niall thought 'twas best, as Ru watched them gather to ride off. The chieftain didn't allow his gaze to land on his daughter, either. The sendoff was silent, uncomfortable, in Niall's estimation.

Ru remained behind while Dunbraith led the small search party. Niall was in no position to question why Ru himself didn't join them, but seeing how daughter and father avoided each other's eyes, Niall was grateful. Most likely, the chieftain didn't trust his actions around his treacherous daughter. Taking the punished Riana with them was awkward for him enough as 'twas. To be scrutinized by her father the entire time as well? Niall breathed a relieved sigh that the giant man remained in the village.

Not that Dunbraith was much better. He was a rigorous taskmaster and had little patience for a weak woman who betrayed her clan. He rode them hard, with Eian and Niall following and several young *Imannae* at the rear. Once they were away from the village wall, Eian rode in the lead, his tracking skills far out-pacing anyone else's of the Caledonii tribe.

And he didn't disappoint. When the first fork in the path appeared, Eian dismounted, crouching close to the mud, and pointed.

"The Roman took that fork. He's headed south."

Brilliant, Riana thought sardonically. Where else would he be headed? Her youngest sister could have told them as much.

They rode in the rain for what seemed like hours, Riana's back screaming in agony as Aila's poultices wore off. Niall had been correct — riding in this weather was misery. Just another part of her punishment.

Several other forks in the trails sent them farther south, Eian's skills at their peak. They had reached the far perimeter of where Roman strongholds near the wall could keep watch, and they slowed their pace, keeping out of sight in the grove of trees.

Dunbraith grumbled the more they rode, and Riana had to bite the inside of her mouth not to smile at the man's ire. Thus far, their ploy had worked. Other than a few inevitable tracks, Horatio was nowhere to be found. And the farther they traveled, the angrier Dunbraith became.

Then the tracks just stopped.

"What do ye mean, stopped?" Dunbraith growled as he leapt off his horse to join Eian on the damp ground. He threw an irate glare at Riana, as if she knew where Horatio hid, before reaching Eian.

Thick growth of grasses and brush lined the path under the trees. And Riana could see it from where she sat. One light footprint, then nothing. Horatio's tracks ended abruptly — almost as though he flew up to the treetops from where he once stood. This time Riana did smile.

As the men scrambled and argued in confusion, Riana lifted her gaze to the leafy trees that shook under the splatter of rain. *Had he taken to the tree boughs?* she wondered. Her eyes shifted to the muddy path. *Or did he use the brush, climbing above to mask his tracks?*

Either way, the Roman's trail was lost, and Dunbraith was haranguing poor Eian.

'Twas then Riana heard a *thunk* sound, and Niall fell off the horse. He landed in the splattering mud in a plaid heap.

"Niall!" she screamed, and Dunbraith, Eian, and the *Imannae* scrambled toward her.

"What happened?" Dunbraith demanded as Eian reached for Niall.

A sudden flurry of spears and arrows flung at them, landing soundlessly. The *Imannae* still on their horses fled. One had been struck by an arrow and, like Niall, dropped to the earth.

Dunbraith was also in a heap on the ground, a worn spear near him. *Was he hit?* she thought stupidly as she grappled for the reins.

Where is Eian? was her next thought as she tugged at the reins that had become entangled in Niall's footwear.

Just as she unwound the leather strap and sat up to urge the horse on, something landed on her head in a painful strike, and all went black.

Chapter Thirteen: Running for His Life

HORATIO RAN LIKE his very life was on fire.

The hardest part was waiting, hoping he'd found the perfect moment. He cringed at the clanking of his chains when he had unlocked them, but the relief when his ragged ankles were freed was worth the scare. The malodorous scent of dead skin and blood assaulted his nose and made his stomach roil. And that was after only a few months?

Putting the foul odor and strange sensation of his ankles from his mind, Horatio scrambled to the wall and with a firm grip on the maddock, he swung it at the remaining daub of the wall. It shattered away in crumbling pieces, and the path to freedom awaited on the other side.

The Maiden of the Storm

Scrambling through the hole, he scanned the yard. 'Twas empty — naught but rain, thunder, and lightening accompanied him. The gods must be on his side now.

No guards called out, no yelling, no spear or hammer striking his backside. No sane person was out in this storm that pounded and shook the ground as though the gods themselves were opening the earth for him.

The heavy wooden bar at the port was most difficult, swollen as it was from the rain. But Horatio smiled to himself — months of lifting boulders prepared his muscles, and he wiggled it from its latch with ease. He slipped around the gate, letting the bolt fall where it may. He was free.

Now it was time to move. Horatio did as Riana had asked and never looked back.

Thunder in the distance kept his pace up, and the lightning overhead lit his way every few minutes. Even with this help, he still tripped over more tree roots, brush, and rocks than he could count. Low branches whipped at his bare ankles. And he couldn't rely on the stars to guide him. Following Riana's dictate to turn left after leaving the port gate, he headed in that southward direction as much as possible.

He had mere hours to reach the wall. In the mud and the dark, falling over obstacles — could he make it? He ran for what seemed like hours. *Too long.* How far had he come?

A cast of blurry light appeared in the distance. Was he imagining it?

Horatio continued in that direction, hoping the incandescent glow meant friends, not foes. Was he at the wall? Or close to it?

He rounded yet another boulder, only to hear words he thought he'd never hear again.

"Halt! Who goes there?" a voice cried out in Latin.

Horatio fell into the arms of a fellow Legion soldier.

"Aetos! Horatio Aetos? What? How —?" The Legionnaire recognized his fellow soldier, missing these past months.

They had been instructed to be on guard and look for him ever since he disappeared. When they had searched for him, they'd found a few drops of blood far on the other side of the wall, but nothing more. Horatio said nothing. He'd cut himself the night he left, falling over a stone when he was drunk. Their superiors had intimated that perchance Horatio had left the army entirely – as a defector.

"We thought you were a deserter!" Marcus admonished as he helped Horatio past the sentry blockade to the surgeon's tent. The damp tents and eagle standards were a welcome sight. Once inside the tent, Horatio collapsed on a pallet in the corner.

'Twas after dawn when Horatio woke, a tingling in his ankles and on the backs of his hands. He lifted his hands to peer at them through bleary eyes.

"Nice to see you awake, soldier," a rough voice commented from the other side of the surgeon's quarters. Horatio turned his head to find the surgeon sitting on a stool and the Legion Prefect standing at attention next to him.

"Once you are recovered, we must have a conversation. The surgeon will send you to my tent as soon as he is satisfied."

Horatio nodded and reclined on his back.

His ordeal may have been over, but the Roman army didn't sleep, and they assuredly wanted retribution for the actions against one of their own. The conference the Prefect called for wouldn't be a pleasant one, Horatio was certain.

The Maiden of the Storm

The camp surgeon gave Horatio a quick appraisal and declared his health sound. Horatio's next stop was the Prefect's tent. A heavy sense of dread clogged Horatio's chest as he pulled on a set of shoe-boots gifted from the surgeon and made his way outside.

The Prefect sat behind a make-shift desk, his thick leather hauberk pressing up against his chin. Horatio, dressed in a new tunic, leggings, and foot coverings that laced tightly up his calves, felt appropriately suited for the first time in months. He stood ramrod straight in front of the Prefect and spun his adventure with the Caledonii.

A secretary in a violent red, draping *paenula* cape scratched copious notes onto rough parchment, and Horatio had to force his eyes from the tunic — the red so resembled Riana's hair that it threatened to take his breath away.

Though Horatio detailed most of the events with acuity, he left out everything as it pertained to Riana and her involvement in his escape. Instead, he said that he pilfered the maddock from the barn and managed to lift the key to the chains from the guard himself. He needed to keep Riana's name from the Roman army, lest she fall victim to any retaliation. Protecting her at all costs was first and foremost in his mind.

"And once you left the village, you headed south until you found us?"

Horatio nodded. "More like fell into you, but aye. That is how I arrived here."

The Prefect never moved his eyes, riveting Horatio in his critical gaze. The secretary bowed, and the Prefect inhaled deeply before speaking again.

"Your service here has been exemplary, and your information will help. Serverus is in Gaul right now, and you are to board a ship in the Rhenish fleet and meet him in Beligca. From there, you will appraise him and deliver this letter, then withdraw to Rome. You've been reassigned as an Urban Cohort to the Praetorian guard."

The Prefect finally dropped his gaze and signed several parchments on the desk.

Horatio froze where he stood, shock over the reassignment rocking him to the core. He'd anticipated coming back to his Legion, perchance even being assigned to Londinium, but not leaving Britannia entirely. He knew nothing of the capital. More importantly, what of Riana? How might he find her, be with her, if he were in Gaul or Rome?

"Domine —" Horatio tried to say, but the Prefect cut him off.

"The ship departs in three days. You will be on it." The Prefect lifted his hard, dark eyes once more. "Dress warm. I hear the sea air is something fierce. Dismissed."

And that was it. After years of service, finding the woman of his dreams, and returning to his men, he was done in Britannia. *Dismissed.*

Horatio turned on his heel and exited the tent, trying to figure out how to stay in Britannia.

Chapter Fourteen: An Ironic Twist of Fate

    RIANA AWOKE WITH her backside in agony and a throbbing headache pounding away at the back of her skull. The cart jounced and swayed, grinding at her bones and making every ache and pain all the worse. She reached up to clasp her head, but her hand didn't move. Instead, a tingling sensation rose from her hands through her arms as she tried to wiggle her fingers. It was then she realized that her hands were bound under her already abused back, going numb from the weight of her body.

    Twisting against her bounds, she flicked her eyes around as far as she could. In the hay and peat filled cart, she counted two other young women and a lad, nay old enough to have hair on his upper lip. One of the *Imannae!* From their positions, they had their hands bound behind them as well.

Riana tipped her head even harder against the boards of the cart, peering at the driver. Two of them sat side by side, their dusky red tunics under leather hauberks telling her everything she needed to know. Romans. She was a Roman captive, and if the stories that coursed amongst the Caledonii were true, she would soon be sent south as a slave.

Oh, the goddesses have a sense of humor.

The irony of her predicament was not lost on Riana. She had helped a Roman slave escape, only to become enslaved by the Romans themselves. Her heart quickened at the thought of her Horatio, a fragile bubble of hope welling in her chest that perhaps Horatio might find her and come to her aid, just as she had saved him.

An unattainable prospect, but a necessary one. Riana needed to cling to any chance of hope if she were to keep her wits about her.

She scooted next to Bevan, the *Imannae* from her tribe. He sighed into her, sharing his worry and fear in the aura that surrounded him.

"I thought ye dead," were his first words, and Riana was grateful he was wrong.

"I feel as though I am," Riana admitted, keeping her voice low. "Do ye ken what happened to the others?"

Bevan shook his russet-brown head. "I saw Dunbraith go down, and Niall. I dinna ken if they are dead or no'. Eian may have been able to ride off with the other *Imannae*, but I was knocked from my mount afore I could see where they went. I dinna see them here, so I believe they escaped."

Riana searched those in the cart with her, but other than the two lasses, 'twas no sign of any other Caledonii from their village. She held onto the same faith as Bevan, that they had escaped.

"Will we be rescued?" the *Imannae* asked, his voice pinched with fear. Riana wished she had a more promising answer.

"I dinna ken. We must hope for the best."

She wondered if she'd be able to take her own advice. Hope seemed very far away.

They bounced along for a while, heading east. Riana glanced to the other women who clung to each other. Perchance they hailed from the same village?

"I am Riana Blogh, daughter of Ru Blogh of the Caledonii," she told them. "Who are ye?"

The lass with darker hair raised her frightened eyes to Riana.

"I am Iona MacPhoil, and this is my sister, Isolde. We are daughters of Heuil MacPhoil."

"Ye are quite a distance from home," Riana acknowledged. The MacPhoil Caledonii village was farther north. "How did ye get here?"

"My sister and I were in the woods, too far from the village, I guess, and we came upon these Roman soldiers." The young woman's voice dropped as she spoke. "I feared they'd have their way with us. Instead they bound our hands and threw us in this cart. I did no' think the Romans took Caledonii as slaves anymore?"

Riana pursed her lips. Peace had been a tentative accord between the Romans and the Caledonii. If the Romans sought to assert their authority, to try reconquering Caledonii, taking chattel might accomplish that. Just as she had warned her father months ago. Riana sighed, dismissing her aggravation. 'Twere more pressing matters at hand.

"I do no' ken why they took us. Who kens why the Romans do anything they do? But there is a chance some men from my village escaped capture. They will reign hell down on the Romans who captured the daughter of Ru."

Riana spoke with an authority she didn't feel. Her eyes kept flicking to the east, wondering why they weren't riding south. That could only mean they were already heading toward the shore.

Her back ached from leaning against the wood of the cart, and she shifted, attempting to take her mind off the spreading throb. Bevan moved over, making more room against the peat, and she tried to rest. Something in the back of her mind cautioned that she was going to need her strength once they arrived at wherever the Romans were taking them.

～

She was dozing against Bevan when the cart jounced awkwardly and the surrounding sounds changed. The ache in her back had spread to her arms and hands, pulsing against her bindings. Whatever their final destination may be, Riana hoped they arrived soon, if for no other reason than to spare her poor hands.

Rotating her head around, she squinted into the horizon. The ground had grown stonier and the air lighter — no longer the heady, earthy scent of heather and the moors. The mist masked her view. Everything in front of the cart faded into the gray.

She adjusted her position again, trying to relieve the ache in her back and arms, when another noise rose above the clanking of the wheels against the stones. The closer they came, the louder the sound grew — a roaring crash in the damp air.

Riana noted the expanse of opaque mist before them where the land ceased to exist. 'Twasn't a trick of the mist. She blinked at a spike of wood, as bare as a tree in winter but draped in swaths of fabric, that rose from the gray. Riana's heart dropped to the pit of her stomach.

A ship.

The Romans were putting them on a ship. If they traversed the sea, they weren't just going south. They were leaving the Highlands altogether, and her father would never find her. She'd be trapped forever.

Riana tried to curb the pulsing panic that rose in her chest. Her breathing came strong and fast, and her whole body shook. Why did they want to remove her from her Highlands? Didn't their Roman cities in southern Britannia need servants? Where were they bound?

The cart drew to a jerking stop at a long set of planks extending into the gray, what Riana now knew to be the northern sea the Caledonii called *Morimaru*, the "dead sea."

An appropriate name. Riana felt as though she was riding to her doom.

The Roman drivers leapt from the cart, and Riana strained to listen in on their conversation. Other Romans appeared from the mist, crimson ghosts from the nether. They spoke in their Latin language, one Riana didn't understand, so her eavesdropping was for naught.

Then the Romans approached the edge of the cart, hauling them forcefully to the planks. Riana landed on her hands at her back and thought she'd pass out from the searing spear of pain. Shaking it off as best she could, she was lifted to her shaky feet and dragged down the deck to the side of the galley ship.

They walked Bevan up the planking first, then Riana, followed by the dark-haired sisters. Bevan tried to fight, pulling and wrestling with his captors, but a sharp strike to his chin quelled his actions. Riana took notice and didn't struggle. She

The Maiden of the Storm

didn't want to add a bruised jaw to her ever-growing list of injuries.

The Romans led them below deck to a low-ceilinged bilge. The wooden ceiling was low enough that Riana's head nearly brushed the damp wood, and Bevan had to duck with the soldiers as they entered.

Rusty chains extended from the far wall of the hold, and one of the soldiers cut her bindings to place her hands in the chains. At least her arms were shackled in front of her this time, and she grimaced as the feeling came back to her fingers in a burning rush.

Riana shivered in the moldy, dank hold. She'd lost her *arasaid* at some point. Her *léine* was thin flax cloth, her summer dress, and this close to the sea, the air held a wet, biting chill. The chattering of her teeth echoed in the cramped space, until Bevan unclasped his *breacan* and, scooting near Riana, tossed the plaid over them both. There they shared body heat, waiting for whatever might happen to them next.

~

Which was not much.

The Romans had not planned on leaving right away, if their lack of movement were any indication.

Their long wait caused a pale light of hope to swell in Riana's chest — that perchance their loitering meant her father and the Caledonii could ride to the shore and find her stuffed in this galley. And though she held onto this thin wisp of hope, she daren't speak it aloud, for fear that she would tempt fate by doing so. Rather, she remained quiet, keeping her thoughts to herself, sending prayers to the goddesses for her and her cohorts' rescue.

The lassies, however, chatted in low voices that carried to Riana and Bevan. As tight as the quarters were, 'twas difficult not to overhear. The one who spoke in the cart, Iona, appeared to be the older sister, and she was trying to put her younger sister's fears to rest.

"Dinna fret, Isolde. We may well be rescued yet. And we are together, if naught else." Iona's voice was like a chant, one she obviously had used often to soothe the younger Isolde throughout their youth. Her sing-song tone worked, and Isolde relaxed as much as she could into Iona's side.

Riana didn't hide her stares. She was at once jealous that the sisters were together — what would she give to have one of her dear sisters to help hold her against her fears? — and resented the woman's words. The lies that spilled from Iona's lips dripped with poisoned honey. Riana's heart held hope, but her mind was sound. She understood the harsh predicament in which they were cast, and being together only made that harrowing situation worse. Could either sister survive, live with herself, if something happened to the other? The thought sent a chill down her spine.

Turning her eyes, she gazed at the young *Imannae's* light brown head that rested on her shoulder. Bevan dozed, clinging to Riana for warmth, and as much as she hated herself for it, she was grateful at least one of her tribe was with her. Poor Bevan. Her gaze cast back to the sisters cuddling in their chains next to her. Poor all of them.

A clanking at the top of the rickety stairwell returned them to full awareness, and all four of them lifted their heads with interest. The Romans spoke in their clipped language as they brought another two young men down the stairs. They were both blonde with fearful eyes and didn't appear to be Caledonii. If not painted Celts, then where did these young men come from?

The Romans chained the two lads to the other edge of the hold and left just as abruptly as they had appeared. The young blond men, a mix of dread and impotent anger emanating from them in a black aura, regarded the others in the hold.

"Where do ye hail from?" Riana asked, breaking the horrible creaking silence.

The first lad only narrowed his eyes, as though 'twas somehow Riana's fault they found themselves on a Roman galley. The other, the lad with softer features, answered.

"I am Duncan. This is my close kin, Arin. We are Otadini."

To Riana's ear, he spoke in a slightly accented Gaelic, a sign of those who lived closer to the western shores. Riana nodded at his answer.

"I am Riana, daughter of Ru Blogh, of the Caledonii to the north. 'Tis Bevan here with me, and over there is Iona and her sister, Isolde."

They took a brief moment to acknowledge each other before Riana continued.

"How did ye come to be here?"

The blond lads glanced at one another before Duncan spoke again.

"The Romans, they are like pirates, raiding the tribes for supplies, for slaves, for whatever they can gain for the 'glory of Rome.'" Duncan spat on the ground at the words.

Wide-eyed, Riana shared shocked looks with the others in the hold.

"But, we are supposed to be at peace with the Romans! What—?"

"Nay, no' in the west and south," Duncan shook his head. "Here, there is no such thing as peace. Ye Highlanders, the painted barbarians, as the Romans call ye, they have yet to breach your defenses. Your tribes give us southern tribes hope that we may one day chase these Roman devils from our land."

Riana sat back, letting Duncan's words sink in. Was this why her father had taken Horatio? He must have known that the peace in the north was tentative, a lie even. To permit the Romans too much latitude was to hand her tribe over to them. Ru and Dunbraith were fighting to keep the Caledonii free. And because of her actions, they had walked right into the clutches of the Romans. No wonder her father was so affronted at what she had done.

Abashed, she lowered her eyes, studying the plaid Bevan shared with her. The *Imannae* was only here because of her rash behavior, and she'd never forgive herself for that.

"Are there others, like us?" Iona asked.

"Enslaved ye mean?" Duncan confirmed. "Aye. The Romans take us when we are alone, away from our tribes, one or two at a time."

"And they've been doing this the whole time?" Riana asked, disbelieving.

Duncan raised his chained hands at her.

"What? Ye think they keep shackles in the galleys for the sheep or linens they transport?"

Riana searched the rest of the hold. Three other sets of irons glinted in the shadows, wolves waiting to capture their prey. Riana shivered again, but not from the cold this time.

Later that day, or night — Riana had lost track of any time in the depths of the ship — a Roman entered with a tray that held dented metal bowls and dry bread. A leather waterskin dangled from the girdle at his hip.

With a lazy hand, the soldier set the bowls before each of them, spilling what little soup remained. He then dropped the hunks of bread and the skin of water with *quaich* cups on the filthy, damp boards, then departed without a sound.

Bevan tossed a few pieces of bread to Duncan and Arin, then tore his in half and handed it to Riana.

"What is this?" she asked, holding up her own hunk. "I have bread."

"Aye," Bevan answered, "but ye are Ru's daughter. I will no' have the daughter of my tribe's chieftain starve."

Bevan's words hit her like a hammer in the chest. He was only here because of her; now he was giving up his sustenance so she might eat. And he said it so casually. The sharp sting of bile rose in the back of her throat.

"I dinna think I can eat what I have, let alone yours, Bevan. My belly has no' stopped jumping since we arrived. Please, eat your food while ye have it."

Bevan kept his earnest hazel gaze on her face as he set his bread next to her bowl. "Save it, then."

"I'll eat it," the once sullen Arin piped up. "I am no' one to give up bread, especially when we dinna ken when we will eat again."

Riana made to grasp her bread, intending to give it to him. Bevan stayed her hand.

"I ken ye may be hungry, but Riana will need to eat once her stomach settles. Eat your own food."

The hard edge to Bevan's voice surprised Riana, and Arin sat back, his attention returning to his own vittles. Bevan was well on his way to becoming the pride of Caledonii warriors.

"Bevan—" she started.

"Eat when ye can, Riana," he commanded.

Then Bevan leaned against the bulkhead, and they ate in tense silence, listening to the lapping waves against the hull of the ship.

Chapter Fifteen: A Surprise on the Ship

HORATIO BOARDED THE worn-looking galley with trepidation. The ship appeared as though it might sink as it crossed a stream, let alone the temperamental North Sea. Gray skies and angry clouds to the west did little to offer any further reassurance. Horatio grimaced at the weather. He couldn't dispel the sense of dread the vessel stirred within him as he mounted the plank that led to the deck.

The galley had sat docked for several days while supplies were loaded. He wasn't the only one reassigned south, and while many soldiers who were pleased with the news wore absurd grins — hoping for warmer climes, no doubt — Horatio didn't share their sense of exuberance. Stepping onto the weather-worn decking, he chanced a look back over his shoulder into the subdued green horizon.

He was leaving a whole world behind here. At least, that's how he felt deep in his heart. His strange, star-crossed emotion for the flaming-haired beauty — one he traveled miles and miles to finally meet — pulled at his chest. How could he leave when everything inside him was pleading with him to stay?

The answer came in the form of a shove. Marcus stood on the plank behind him, not looking where he was going nor seeming to care. He hit Horatio's back with a solid thump, and Horatio tottered on the edge of the plank. Marcus grabbed Horatio's tunic to help him regain his balance.

"Are you in such a rush to get on that galley? It looks as though it can barely stay afloat!" Horatio said.

Marcus snickered. "'Tis a sight better than landing face-first in that water. Have you been swimming in the North Sea, Horatio? 'Tis like a never-ending winter. Icy, just above freezing. I'd not want my worst enemy to end up swimming in these shores. Can you not feel the spray?"

Horatio glanced down as he continued mounting the plank, low waves lapping against the ship. The chill in the air alone was enough to convince him Marcus was correct. He didn't need to feel the spray off the sea. If the air was this cool and damp at the height of summer, how cold was that water? Horatio didn't want to find out.

His trepidation returned on the heels of that thought. If that heap of a ship didn't stay afloat, they would each enjoy an icy dip in the sea.

Adjusting his pack, Horatio stepped onto the rickety galley with leaden feet.

The only bright spot to this journey was that one day he may return, and when he did, he vowed to stop at nothing to find Riana.

The Maiden of the Storm

Horatio was surprised when one of the other soldiers who led him to his bunk under the top deck mentioned they'd been moored for the past three days. From what Horatio remembered of the shipbuilder's conversations back home, the Roman *Liburnians* became waterlogged and needed to be pulled out of the sea for a time. Presumably, the crew knew this — why had they remained docked for so long? A prickle of wariness made the hairs on the back on his neck rise, and he surveyed the already derelict ship with a more discerning eye.

The construction of a galley was further compromised if green wood was used in the building process. Horatio's mind didn't stop as his eyes searched, catching every gap and warped plank of timber on the *Liburnian*. And the storm that was approaching? 'Twas the trifecta of quandaries. These aspects seemed to point to a significant problem for the ship, and for those on it.

"Here," the soldier said as he waved his hand at the rope bed swinging from the posts. "And you can lay your pack there, on the ledge. When you're done, come to the top deck to help with the rigging. You've the muscles for it."

A wry smile tugged at Horatio's mouth. Of course, he had the muscle for it. Months of hefting boulders packed muscle on anyone. But it would feel good to put his strength to use. Horatio had never been a lay-about.

He placed his pack where the soldier directed and threw his *sagum* cape over the bed, hoping it was more comfortable than it looked. Lifting himself onto the swaying bed, Horatio nestled in the ropes. Curled up in his heavy cape with the gentle rocking, he sensed sleep would come easily. 'Twas *quite* comfortable.

A crashing from above drew him from his reverie, and he fumbled from the bed, grabbed his cape, and headed toward the steps. The space below deck was cramped enough, but at least he wasn't sleeping amongst animals and cargo. Those were housed in the lower hold under his, the grate leading to those steps visible as he climbed into the chilly air above deck. Marcus met him at the top of the ladder.

"We have a bit to do afore we leave," he said, tossing a hemp rope the width of Horatio's forearm at him. Horatio caught it.

"I thought we were leaving right after we climbed aboard?" Horatio asked.

He flicked his eyes to the westward horizon as he spoke. The clouds grew more tempestuous, harrowing, even, and Horatio wondered if they would try to outrun the storm. Though, from the looks of the galley ship, Horatio doubted the efficacy of that plan. Thunder cracked in the distance, and Horatio shuddered. They should have left hours ago. If the storm was as fearsome as it appeared in the horizon, this ship might well end up as nothing more than water-logged debris washing ashore.

"It takes a bit to get a ship moving. We don't just climb aboard and sail. You should know that. Once the rigging and rowers are in place, we'll shove off. Now, are you going to help me with this rope or not?"

Horatio lifted the rope and followed Marcus across the deck, pulling his cape more tightly around him as they went.

They still hadn't departed as the sky darkened and rain pattered on the deck. A centurion seized Marcus and Horatio, ordering them to climb to the kitchen galley below and gather foodstuffs for the chattel in the hold.

"Chattel?" Horatio asked, wondering what manner of animals were being removed from the Highlands. Those furry cows? The raggedy, woolly sheep?

Marcus shrugged in response and dipped his head, doing his duty. Marcus was an exemplary soldier that way, never questioning a superior's commands.

Horatio's attention was far too focused on the inclement weather — the skies were now black, and a deluge of rain had opened from the skies and battered the ship. He followed Marcus blindly into the hold.

At the back of his mind, he pondered why they were getting food for the chattel in the bottom deck at the galley. *Wouldn't the hay or water suffice for the animals in the hold? Hadn't they already been fed?* Maybe some smaller animals needed attention.

His breath froze in his chest when he watched Marcus gather the tray of vittles from the cooks in the galley. Horatio clasped the leather skin of water thrust at him without realizing what his hands were doing.

This was not food for chattel animals. This was sustenance for people — for slaves. A hollow sensation overwhelmed him as he stood stupidly in the galley.

Slaves? We are transporting slaves? Horatio knew that ships in the south, in and around the Mediterranean, transported defeated peoples to Rome to serve as servants and slaves, but this far north? With an undefeated people? During a time of peace? That hollow sensation in his chest grew.

Having been enslaved for the past few months — living that horror, even as his capture was almost light compared to stories he'd heard in the army — and knowing slaves were on this boat, came as a harsh slap in the face. He knew slavery hadn't end with his escape, but to see that horror now on his ship, under his feet, Horatio wasn't sure he could accept those conditions, to support their upkeep.

He well understood Riana's inherent and vehement dislike for the practice.

Watching Marcus carry the meager platter of stew and bread from the galley, Horatio struggled with what to do. Protest? To whom? Who, other than Horatio, had a care for any ethical or moral plight of the prisoners? Finally, he moved, following Marcus to the ladder that led to the lowest deck. Horatio was one man in an empire that spanned the entire world — what could he possibly do to halt a custom in practice since the beginning of time?

Resigned, Horatio shook his head to clear it and stepped into the dank recesses of the darkened hold.

The all-too familiar and bone chilling clanking of shackles and chains welcomed them as they reached the lowest deck. Those unfortunate souls in irons cowered deep in the shadows, buried as it were, against the stern of the ship. The grinding and creaking were worse in here, where the water battled against the dripping hull and appeared to be winning.

Marcus pointed behind the ladder. "Leave the skin here and go water the goats back there. Then give the others their water."

Horatio hadn't noticed the din of bleating goats emanating from the far side of the hold behind the ladder. He tossed a few handfuls of hay to the goats and made sure they had their bowls filled from the water barrel against the hull. Then he turned his attention to Marcus and his endeavors.

Marcus had flung the bread on the filthy, damp floor and left bowls of watery stew, if it could even be called that, by their feet. Grabbing the oak *quaich* cups left from the morning, Marcus tossed them to Horatio one at a time. Horatio juggled them before setting each on the ladder step to fill.

He handed four of the cups back to Marcus, then brought the remaining two over to set them by the slaves himself.

Horatio didn't make a full step before he dropped the cups on the ground, his jaw hanging open at who sat chained to the hull.

'Tis a joke, Horatio tried to convince himself, shaking his head. *Either that or the salty air is playing tricks with my eyes.*

But who else had that vibrant swath of hair or pale green eyes that could pierce the darkness?

In the background, he heard Marcus mock him for his clumsiness. But the voice didn't penetrate any further. Everything in his body and mind focused on the woman sitting dejectedly before him.

How did she get here? What happened after I left? Had the Roman army managed to breach the Caledonii tribes north of the wall?

His thoughts swam in a harsh rush, tinged with shock. When he eventually spoke, his voice was little more than a harsh whisper in the dark.

"Riana?"

Chapter Sixteen: How to Take Advantage of a Bad Situation

HER EYES WERE bleary. Her entire body ached from lack of movement and cold, and Riana barely registered the Romans who entered with their evening meal. Rolling thunder outside the galley attracted most of her attention. She knew where they were on this ship — the lowest deck. If anything happened to these warped boards . . . if the storm was too much or the waves too violent . . .

"Riana?"

She shifted her head, trying to focus her gaze on the soldiers who brought their evening meal. At least, that was the meal Bevan told her was forthcoming, and since his faculties seemed more intact than hers, she was wont to believe him.

The man directly in front of them was unfamiliar — a shorter Legionnaire with dusty brown hair pasted to his low-browed forehead from the rain.

She moved her sights to the other man.

And her heart dropped to the pit of her stomach.

What? How? She was certain her eyes deceived her and blinked several times to clear her vision.

It wasn't possible.

Was that Horatio?

Riana crept forward a few inches, trying to get a better view of the soldier before her. Tall, dark-haired, and well-muscled. Suddenly the wide-eyed man stiffened, shaking his head imperceptibly. She may have been agitated, but she knew a signal when she saw one.

Especially when it came from Horatio.

He wanted her to feign that she didn't know him.

Riana didn't know how to react. She wanted to rush him, as much as her shackles allowed, feel him hold her chilled body in his strong, warm embrace. She wanted him to tell her that he was here to rescue her. It took every ounce of will power to remain seated with her eyes downcast.

Horatio's dark face hardened to a mask of shadows when the other soldier spoke. She didn't understand what the Roman said, but Horatio answered in his language, then picked up the cups and refilled the water.

Placing the cups before the sisters to Riana's right, Horatio hid his eyes, pretending he didn't know her.

Riana mimicked his disinterest, fascinated with her meal. She knew what his signal had meant. 'Twas dangerous if any Romans realized they had a shared history. If the soldiers learned she'd been a part of Horatio's imprisonment, she could only imagine what punishments they would endure.

Nay, she didn't want to imagine.

Horatio retreated with his fellow Roman up the ladder without a backward glance, the cringing sound of the hatch above closing, sealing them in captivity once more.

Riana's eyes remained on her bowl of watery stew, trying to make sense of what just happened. Shock at seeing Horatio shook her to her bones.

They ate in silence for several moments before one of the cousins spoke.

"What was that all about?" asked Arin, his stern face focused on Riana.

Riana flicked her gaze in his direction but didn't answer. She sipped at the tepid liquid in the bowl.

"Did that Roman ken ye?" Arin pressed.

Bevan cut the cousin an angry glare, ready to intervene, but Riana stayed him with a light touch. Keeping her gaze averted, she swallowed before responding.

"I think I saw him above deck. Some men are taken aback by my coloring, especially when I have stripes of woad on my cheeks."

"Ye dinna wear the woad now," his cousin, Duncan, piped up.

"I dinna ken the man," Riana answered, her tone indicating she was done discussing the Romans.

The cousins shared a look before returning to their meal.

"I think ye are lying," Arin said under his breath.

Regardless, everyone in the hold heard him.

∽

A bustling of activity clattered above them, echoing into the bulkhead below. The soldiers were readying to set sail. The ship would depart, leaving behind the only home Riana had ever known.

She blinked back hot tears.

The sound of the rain whipping against the hull, combined with the turbulent waves that battered the waterlogged *Liburnian*, meant the storm was well upon them. She sent a prayer up to the goddesses that the ship could withstand the assault.

Another crash of thunder made Riana jump against Bevan, who sat rigid along the weeping planks of the hold. More water. An impossible amount. Riana had a frightening idea that they were not going to make it across the sea this day, or any. None of what had transpired in the past few days boded well.

Bevan relaxed when Riana settled into his side to rest. They jerked hard as a deep creaking sound ground in their ears.

"He is right," Bevan said in a hushed tone, directly in her ear. He didn't want anyone else to overhear. "Ye are lying. That Roman, he was our prisoner, aye? The one Ru caught near the wall?"

Bevan may have been young, but he wasn't stupid. His breath was warm on her face as he waited for her answer. Not that she needed to respond in the least. The lad had the right of it.

"Aye," she whispered back, not wanting the sisters or the cousins to hear.

She couldn't have them trading that knowledge for favors. Iona and Isolde may not think of it, but the cousins, Duncan and Arin, might leap at the opportunity to improve their circumstances if it presented itself.

"If ye did help him escape, Riana," Bevan kept his voice low so only Riana could hear him, "do ye think he will do the same? Is he that type of man?"

Riana believed him to be that manner of man — she knew it to the depths of her soul. But what possible difference could Horatio make? And once they were at sea, away from the Highlands, they might as well be in Rome itself. 'Twould be impossible to find their way home.

Another crack of thunder made her jump, and she leaned into Bevan.

"If he can, he will," she said.

Bevan nodded curtly, accepting her answer. Though, even Riana wasn't sure she believed her own words.

The *Liburnian* had scarcely cast off the docks when the skies opened in a full deluge, sheets of rain and bolts of lightning driving the men for cover. Soldiers abandoned their posts, leaving the rigging to run amok and the sails to flap uselessly in the sharp winds.

Horatio held his breath. The ship was the scene of a disaster. Many a ship had been torn apart in storms, and even close to land, whole navies had been lost when smashed against the rocks. The waves lobbed the galley like a toy, and fear welled in Horatio's chest.

Not for himself, but for his red-haired goddess chained below. What if the ship took on sea water? How could he get them out of those chains? Could he give Riana and the other captives an opportunity if the boat smashed to pieces in the sea?

She had saved him — given him back a life he thought long gone. The most amazing gift. Now this storm may offer him the chance to save her. Return her gift, if he could just figure out a way.

Another round of lightning and thunder sent the men on deck into a frenzy. Then, before he could make a move, a soldier rushed up from the lower deck, his face a mask of pure panic.

"The galley! On fire!"

Nothing was worse than a fire on a ship. With nowhere to go, and only the frightening depths of the sea below, a fire was a death threat for all on board. The singular goal typically was to extinguish the flames and save the crew, but that crew was too busy battling the storm threatening its own devastation to the galley.

A fire inside the ship. A storm on the outside. The men in chaos. It was the perfect trifecta of opportunity.

Horatio's mind raced. Grabbing a line of loose rigging, he left Marcus sniveling near the bow of the ship and made his way toward the hatch that led below deck. The ship tossed amongst the waves, listing dangerously starboard. With the deck sopping wet, the boards were slick, and Horatio's grasp on the rigging was not enough for him to keep his balance.

He slid across the deck, his fingers scratching for purchase on the slippery wood as he glided past the hatch. One finger caught the metal lattice of the hatch and twisted. Horatio clenched his jaw, wiping at his dripping eyes. The digit was broken, undoubtedly.

Ignoring the throbbing pain from his fingertip, Horatio used his other hand to lift the hatch, only to be welcomed by an intense rush of heat and plume of smoke. The force of it drove him back a step, but Horatio pushed forward, past the scorching space that battled the chilly air of the storm. Bracing himself against the blaze, Horatio descended into the smoky darkness.

Fortunately, the damp had limited the fire to the kitchen galley. Only small flames licked at the steps, and those were weak at best. The sounds down below, though, were the stuff of nightmares. If the hull hadn't cracked from the brutality of the waves, then the fire would weaken it.

Another burst of thunder and screaming above deck made Horatio pause. He looked up at the wooden beam overhead. The shrieking grew louder, and Horatio guessed the lightning struck the rigging mast, either splintering it or catching it aflame. He hadn't heard the decimating crack yet, so it hadn't fallen. He still had time.

❧

When he had brought food down with Marcus just a short time ago, he'd caught the movement of Marcus's hand from the corner of his eye. The key to the hatch?

The hazy smoke thickened as he passed the galley, combing the floorboards for the hatch lost in the haze. Coughing into the smoky air, he dropped to his knees, feeling for the hatch itself.

Once his fingers snared the lattice of the hatch, he then trailed his fingers around the edges, hissing at the pain of his fingertip and searching for the post where it seemed Marcus had grabbed the keyring.

He struck his head against a post as he searched, seeing stars before he regained his senses. Between the ship tossing in the storm and the heady, burning stench of smoke, he struggled to keep his wits. Everything inside him screamed to leave, to find the top deck and save himself.

Battling against that instinct, he reached his hand around the post and heard the jingle of iron as his finger brushed against the keys.

Confidence surged through him, giving him the boost he needed to suppress his wretched desire to flee and focus on the urgent task facing him.

Four keys dangled from the ring, and the third one he tried worked, slipping the lock from its place. He swung open the hatch, the cool air from below offering a moment of reprieve for his aching chest. Inhaling the cleaner air of the hold, he stumbled down the steps.

"Riana!" he coughed into the darkness. His eyes burned, and he squinted to see in the recesses below deck.

"Here!" her bold voice called out. "We are over here!"

Chapter Seventeen: Limited Options

ONCE THE SHIPPED jerked, indicating they were adrift at sea, the pounding of the waves against the hull increased. They battered the flimsy galley, nearly drowning out the sounds of the storm wreaking havoc above. The ship creaked and groaned around them, and Riana was certain she heard a splintering sound at the aft joist.

Panic smothered her in a heavy blanket, and though she tried to mask her fright, Bevan read it on her face.

"Aye, I heard it, too," Bevan confirmed.

The ship may stay afloat even if it sprung a leak or worse, the hull was breached — the galley still might not sink — but that wouldn't stop the hold from flooding, or the ship from breaking into pieces. Then it wouldn't matter if they survived any flooding or not. They'd perish in the sea. 'Twas valid reasoning behind the name *Morimaru*.

Low cooing sounded from her right, where Iona was singing a chanting song to her sister who clung to her in desperation. Even the animals on the far side of the ladder seemed to notice, bleating with more intensity and pawing at the ground. The captives in the hold may not have been aware of the pressure the hull was under, but even a non-seafarer well understood when a situation was precarious.

And their situation, chained to the very hull that threatened to burst, was precarious indeed.

Bevan leaned into Riana as far as their chains permitted, trying to offer her a modicum of support. And while it didn't calm her in any way, she was grateful for the attempt and reclined into Bevan to return the favor.

The sharp cracking noise surprised them both, causing everyone in the hold to jump away from the hull. The seam in the hull finally gave way, leaking water in a weak spray. All eyes focused on the sea water, understanding just how dire their position was. Isolde began to weep, hiding her face in her sister's kirtle. Riana knew how she felt. She wanted to do the same.

"What now?" Arin asked from across the hold. Riana turned her fretful gaze to his. "Want to admit the truth about the Roman, now? Mayhap he can help us here. Otherwise, we shall become one with the sea."

His flat voice hid any sign of fear or worry, and his cousin elbowed him in the ribs.

"Arin!" he reprimanded, but Arin just shrugged him away. His dire expression never left Riana.

A disturbance on the steps interrupted the tense moment. A ragged and stained Horatio spilled down the ladder into the dampness of the hold. He found his footing and peered into the shadows. A set of keys dangled from his hand.

The Maiden of the Storm

"Riana?" he called out.

"Here! We are over here!"

The boat shifted and Horatio tripped his way to Riana, crouching to her.

"What's going on, Horatio? Why are ye here?"

"The ship is in distress. Lightening hit a sail, I think, and a small fire has broken out in the galley. And this storm is going to rip this boat to pieces. We are still close enough to land that we may make it if we can swim or find a float. But not with these chains. . ."

His voice trailed off as he held up the thick iron keys.

"I know these will sever you from the hull, but as for the shackles around your wrists , . . ." he trailed off again, leaving the implication hanging.

But of course, the key to their wrist chains had to be on the keyring, didn't it?

Horatio reached around Riana to the wall and unlocked their manacles, then did the same for Iona and her sister, and the two cousins.

Arin raised a judgmental eyebrow. "Dinna ken the man, eh?" he asked as his chains fell from the iron link set into the wood.

With a rising sense of urgency, Horatio tried each of the keys on the chains binding Riana to Bevan, cursing under his breath and shaking with every crash of thunder.

None worked. He tried the keys on the sisters and the cousins, to no avail.

"How are we supposed to swim ashore when we are bound? We are doomed if we try!" Riana tried to contain the panic in her voice and failed.

"'Tis better to remain on the ship than drown in chains," Duncan spoke what they all were thinking. The heavy iron, acting like an anchor, would drag them to their watery deaths at the bottom of the sea.

"No, not if we have something to help you float. I can swim and tug you toward shore."

He scanned the room, noting barrels tucked beneath the steps. He raced over and maneuvered one through the hull, rotating it back and forth across the wet floor. Horatio hadn't missed the leak in the seam.

"We can use these."

It was a desperate, impossible plan. It was also the only plan. What other option was open to them? None.

"That's all well, but are we to carry the barrels up the steps and just meander off the ship? Even in this chaos, I can no' believe your soldiers will let us try to escape." Arin gave them a flat expression. He appeared resigned to their impending death.

Horatio opened his mouth to answer when the hatch above crashed. They spun toward the ladder to see a soldier, a centurion commander from the looks of his tunic, hurry down the steps.

"Soldier! What are you doing down here! We need you above to help —" The centurion stopped short, regarding the group standing near the center of the hull.

"What are you doing?" the centurion asked in a skeptical voice, stepping toward Horatio.

"Bringing the slaves mid-deck. There's a leak," Horatio pointed to the seam, "and I've been tasked to bring them and the animals above deck."

"Tasked by who?" The centurion squinted at Horatio. "All hands are needed on the main deck to help with the rigging and sails so we can ride out the storm. You should be there. This chattel is of no consequence."

"No, I —" Horatio started, looking around the hull, and shrugged at Riana.

The Maiden of the Storm

Then he faced the centurion and struck him solidly in the jaw with a hammer fist.

The centurion stumbled back with a mix of shock and pain. Before he could shake off the hit, Horatio launched forward and struck him on the other side of his face. The soldier crumpled to the ground in a heap. Horatio swung around to the chained onlookers and shrugged again at Riana.

"Lifting rocks was good for something. Come on. We need two more barrels. I have an idea."

They heaved and shifted as the ship tossed about in the sea, the waves further ravaging and wearing away the already weakened hull.

Horatio positioned himself directly in front of the leaking seam of the hull, an iron bar that he'd swiped from the animal pen in his hand.

The sisters and the cousins stood behind Riana and Bevan, looks of trepidation plastered on their pale faces. They could only guess at what Horatio had planned for them, and they didn't relish it.

⁓

Thunder raged again, as did another wave against the hull, and the leak sprayed harder, increasing in size. It was only a matter of time before the hull was fully compromised, and the sea came crashing in. An explosive crash sounded from above their heads. Their eyes shifted upward in terrified glances. This time, though, the crash was accompanied by a splintering sound, and the entire ship vibrated.

Horatio whirled around.

"Do you trust me?" His hazel eyes flashed with intensity and urgency, reflecting the chaos of the microcosmic world on the ship.

Riana didn't hesitate.

"Aye."

Horatio nodded once. "Then hold on."

He squeezed the bar into the leak at the seam of the hull and pulled. His dusky muscles from his arms to his chest bulged and flexed, and once again he thanked the gods for his time lifting Caledonii boulders. This task would have been much more difficult, if not impossible, if he didn't have the strength.

The wood screamed in protest. Horatio took a deep breath, trying to ignore the icy spray of water and his aching hand and prepared for the flood that would come next. Then everything seemed to happen at once.

The seam gave way and a rush of frigid water swirled in. Horatio shifted his grip and pulled more of the ragged wood from the top of the opening. The hole needed to be large enough to force everyone past the onslaught of water, and fit the barrels out, and make sure no one drowned in the process. The precarious nature of this plan made Horatio sweat, even as chills from the frigid sea soaked through his leather foot coverings.

When the final board broke off, they jumped back as even more of the North Sea splashed into the ship. The hole in the deck was right above sea level, but not for long. It was obvious to anyone who watched that, no matter what the soldiers or crew did top deck, the ship was doomed.

"Here, help me." Horatio nodded at Riana, who waved at the cousins.

She and Bevan grabbed one side of the barrel, while Duncan and Arin trudged through the ankle-deep rush of water to grab the other side.

The Maiden of the Storm

Horatio led Iona, and they both dragged her squealing sister to the barrel right into the onslaught of seawater.

"No! No, please Iona!" Isolde wiggled, fighting him, but Horatio's grip was too strong.

Iona stood on one side of the barrel, her arms with the chains draped atop and over to her sister. Horatio placed an icy fingertip on Iona's chin. His voice rose loudly enough to be heard under the boat's cracking and the water's roar.

"You must stay with the barrel." He lifted his eyes from Iona's and scanned the room, touching each prisoner's face with his own gaze as he spoke. "The chains are too heavy, and if you slip from the barrel, you will find your death at the bottom of the sea. The barrels will keep you afloat, but only if you stay with them. It may be difficult. The sea is a riot in this storm, but you must stay with the barrel."

His eyes skipped around again, meeting each person who nodded solemnly at his advice. They knew what this endeavor meant. If they remained in the ship, they'd drown, without question. If they escaped with the barrel through the gap in the hull, they had a chance, no matter how slim, to survive.

The chance to live was better than no chance at all.

"I will do my best to direct you back toward land. But you must kick hard, try to swim past the waves, kicking the whole time." He returned his attention to Iona. "Ready?"

"NO, IONA!" Isolde's panicked voice rose to a heart-rending crescendo. "I canna swim! There's lightening! IONA!"

"Shush now, Isolde." Grasping her sister's hand atop the barrel, Iona cooed with her patient speech that marveled Riana. How did she manage to keep so calm a voice during such chaos?

"I will follow you soon," Horatio said in a lower voice that Iona and Riana barely heard over the cacophony. "Go now."

With Riana pushing Iona as the others shoved the barrel, they managed to get both girls and their flotation past the onrush of sea water and into the tumultuous path toward freedom. Isolde's screaming was lost in the waves.

Horatio spun around, his eyes on Riana. She tipped her head at the cousins.

"You are next, young men," Horatio said, turning his attention to the thick blond youths shivering in the hold.

"But what about —" Duncan flicked his chin at Riana who shook her head.

"Nay, ye go. Now."

This time, the cousins didn't argue, but rolled the barrel on its side and positioned themselves. They could help maneuver the barrel through the gap as Horatio, Riana, and Bevan pushed from behind.

With a pop like a strange birth from a poisoned beast, Duncan and Arin burst through the hull and were swallowed up in the sea. Horatio swung around again, this time focused on Riana. He had to get her off this ship of misery, get her to the mainland, at all costs.

Riana stood shivering, watching as the cousins and their only safety against the sea disappeared through the hole.

She'd never been so cold in her life, a painful, bone-biting cold, but it didn't feel real against the fear and desperation that overtook her entire being. That Horatio managed to keep his wits, come up with an escape plan, and execute it amid this frigid debacle, stunned her. Had she been able to think clearly, she might have paused and realized the futility of this mad plan.

As 'twas, she was too cold and too terrified to contradict Horatio. And since 'twas the only plan they had, Riana was going to follow his commands.

The sounds of the chaos above deck and the water in the hold below didn't quite drown out the noise of panicked animals, as their own desperate movements grew louder. They pawed and clawed at their pens, their own survival instincts on high. Riana tilted her head at the pathetic noises, and she noticed that Horatio's head lifted, too. Then his eyes flicked toward the step where his compatriot still lay prone and unconscious.

"Riana, you and the young man. Now." Horatio grabbed her chains, and with encouraged movement from Bevan, draped her over the round of the barrel. "I will follow ye out soon."

"No, wait, Horatio. Come now, please! I don't want to leave ye!"

The panic in her voice shone through her eyes as well, pale green storms that matched the tempest outside. His own eyes held her gaze for a heartbeat.

"You aren't leaving me. I shall join you in the sea. I just need to move them—"

"No!" Riana cried.

"Riana, I can't leave them to suffer and drown. 'Tis no less than what you have done for me."

Riana's whole body broke. "But what if I lose ye again?" Riana's voice echoed with soul-crushing anguish. "I lost ye once. I can no' do that again!"

Horatio's face softened, a stark contrast of peace against the turmoil surrounding them.

"You haven't lost me. I am here for you now. And I will always be here for you. But if we want to live our lives together, you must leave now. I will find you."

Then his surprisingly warm lips were on her shivering, icy ones, capturing her mouth with a promise for a future than might never be. Just as she kissed him back, he yanked his head away.

"I will find you," he vowed again, then shifted his face to Bevan. "Soldier!" Horatio called out and Bevan's head snapped to attention. "Take Riana and bring her to safety. Do not let anything happen to her. And get her out of here now. Can you do that?"

"Aye, sirrah!" Bevan yelled back, his face turning to stone with fierce determination.

Horatio didn't look at Riana again, fearing he might not be able to let her go. He treaded through the rising flood to the rear of the barrel and with Bevan's aide, shoved his love through the gap in the hull. The last of Riana that Horatio saw was her scarlet hair, like blood in the water, coursing out behind them as they paddled into the sea.

Giving himself only a few breaths to compose himself after Riana and Bevan departed the hold, Horatio sprang into action before the cold and exertion overwhelmed him.

The water, now nearly calf deep, slowed him more than he expected. But it made moving the centurion much easier. Horatio floated the prone man to the ladder, then with rough force and trying to protect his injured finger, clamored up to the mid deck. The centurion's body bounced with each wooden step, and Horatio winced as they went. If he survived this ordeal, the soldier might wake to a shocking series of bruises.

Once he made it to the hatch, Horatio lurched with the last bit of his waning strength, hauling the soldier onto the mid deck. The galley fire had appeared to lessen, but the smoke was still painfully thick, and Horatio coughed uncontrollably as he dumped the soldier. The man was out of the flooding hold — it was the best Horatio could do for him.

Wiggling past the man's body, Horatio then leapt down the steps to the animals at the rear of the stairwell. Their panicked cries and bleating increased, and several of the poor animals were already treading water to stay alive.

Grabbing at the key ring on his belt, he tried the keys until one worked the pen latch, and the animals flooded out like the very water that flowed into the hold. Once a few of the beasts made it to the ladder, he knew the rest would follow. It was the best he could do for the animals.

The ship listed, throwing Horatio off balance and face first into the water. He was weakening, most of his energy sapped by getting Riana and the other captives out of the hold. He was reaching the end of his abilities, and he still needed to swim in that storm-raging sea. For a moment, he wanted to lie on the deck and let the water overtake him, but he didn't stop. He couldn't. He'd made a promise, and it was time to keep it.

Rising from the water in a dripping mess, Horatio stripped off as much of his waterlogged and weighty leather as possible. 'Twouldn't do to tell everyone else to be wary of being weighed down only to drown because he forgot to remove his armor.

He waded to the gap in the wood, facing the stream of water. He well understood why everyone had to be pushed out. The view was daunting. Giving the last chance of survival to the sea was a fearsome thing. Then he inhaled as much air as his lungs could hold and dove through the hole and out of the doomed ship.

The Maiden of the Storm

Chapter Eighteen: Seaside Reunions

THE SEA WAS the stuff of nightmares. Riana had never seen such an imposing, frightening sight, and here she was, right in the middle of it.

Waves swept higher than the trees outside her village and crashed with ship-crushing ferocity. She worried those waves might crush the barrel and destroy their life-giving float. Lightening reflected in the water and the air, and thunder shook Riana to her bones. The sky was almost as black as night, as black as the divine Goddess Rhiannon's hair, with a power just as imposing, as though the Goddess herself was destroying her own creation.

Riana sent up a prayer that 'twas not true, that her barrel and she and Bevan on the other side might remain intact. Squinting against the pelting rain, she risked glancing back at the ship, hoping beyond hope that the dusky head of Horatio was floating in the waves. If the storm were the stuff of nightmares, the ship was what the Christians called hell.

The ship's masts were completely gone, the sails spilling over the sides of the ship as useless drapes. Flames licked out from the lower deck onto the upper deck, but the fire was the least of the worries for those still on board.

The jagged holes along the hull, pockmarks in the weathered wood, weakened the entire structure of the *Liburnian* and allowed even more of the sea to batter the ship both inside and out. Men screamed and flung about the deck, and Riana watched in horror as soldiers in full military gear, heavy leather and metal, throw themselves from the railing and sink like anchors. What hope did those poor men have?

The barrel floated them away from the stern of the boat, and Riana shifted her eyes, scanning the sea for a sign, any sign, of Horatio. Nothing but the raging sea and its black waves.

She then twisted her face forward, *since that is the way ye are going,* she said to herself, echoing a life lesson her father had taught her when she was a bairn. *Dinna look back, ye aren't going that way.* Blinking to clear her eyes, she squinted again.

Ahead, bouncing in the waves, Duncan and Arin clung to their barrel with pale, desperate hands. Their heads never turned back, and Riana wondered if they could spot the sisters in front of them. Riana was unable to see anything past the cousins.

Her arms were tired. Her hair stuck to her face in icy ropes. Her shoulders screamed in pain, raised as they were with her arms flung over the barrel round. If it weren't for the chains binding her to Bevan, Riana undoubtedly would have already slipped into the sea. The cold was at once numbing and biting, and she fretted ever feeling her feet again.

And if she were this fatigued just holding onto a barrel, what of Horatio? He worked to get them off the ship, then release the animals to safety. How exhausted was he? Did he have anything to hold onto that might float him to shore? Or was he swimming against this fearsome tide on his own?

Riana sent up another prayer, this one to the Goddess of the Sea and the afterlife, *Chlíodhna*, to protect them from the ravaging sea. And if not that, then to help them reach the land. Riana flicked her eyes over her shoulder once more. Still no sign of Horatio.

～

Horatio was tired. Tired in a way he never imagined possible. Everything in his body cried out to stop, to rest, but he knew if he did that, even for a moment, he was as doomed as the ship behind him. He chanted to himself over and over in his head, *keep going, keep going.*

Swimming in the sea-ravaged waves was a labor that seemed beyond daunting. Just as he managed to get through one set of waves, another crashed down, forcing him underwater. His lungs throbbed from holding his breath and his legs from kicking like a madman to resurface. Then, as he struggled to burst above the water and inhale, another wave crashed, and the entire process repeated.

He feared he'd never reach the shore.

Underwater, he noted, was an easier swim, not having to deal with the crashing as much as managing the rise and fall of each crest. Deciding to take the past of least resistance, Horatio took another deep breath and dove below the surface, swimming as vigorously as his arms permitted before his lungs demanded air, forcing him up to the raging surface again.

Surfacing granted him the opportunity to check his distance, using the ship for perspective. It originally had a bearing of south-southeast, so he hoped that keeping the boat in that general direction behind him meant he was heading toward shore northwest and not, gods-forbid, toward the open sea.

He also didn't see the barrels when he surfaced. Shouldn't he be able to see them by now? Had they made it to shore yet? The ship wasn't too far out to sea when the storm hit, shouldn't he be close?

Horatio needed to change his focus — if he concentrated too much on his weary, aching muscles and frozen hands and feet, he'd never make it to land.

Instead he pictured Riana on that rocky beach, wearing naught but her thin *léine* that billowed around her finely shaped legs. In his mind's eye, her hair glowed in the sunlight, an aura of warmth surrounding her as she held out her hand, inviting him to join her on the rocky beach.

And her eyes, those fierce eyes that rivaled the storm on the sea, beckoned, sultry and filled with desire. Desire for him, his body, his life.

Horatio kept swimming, determined to see those eyes once more.

<hr />

Riana thought she must have passed out. There was no other reason. One moment she was battling the crashing waves, and the next she was washing up to the shore, the barrel breaking within its iron bands against the stones and Bevan dragging her from the icy sea.

She didn't know where she was, if it were the rocky beach of the firth or an isolated island. And she didn't care. Solid land was beneath her frozen feet, and for that she thanked the gods and goddesses.

Then her mind came to her, slowly thawing and waking. She whipped her head around at the stones and lapping waves.

"Horatio?" she croaked out to Bevan. "The sisters? The cousins?"

She and Bevan could not be the only ones who made it, could they? 'Twas not possible to risk so much, to overcome the rages of the sea and storm, only to find that no one else had survived the arduous journey.

A chill not borne of the frigid waters coursed through her. Surely Horatio survived?

"The shore is long, with many inlets. Perchance they landed elsewhere. 'Twas no' a direct path, aye?"

In a stilted pose, Riana nodded. The youthful *Imannae* had the right of it. Leaving the remains of the barrel behind, they started up the rocky shoreline, calling out for the others.

On the other side of a clump of grasses and brush that grew in patches near the lapping waves, they found the Iona and Isolde in fair shape, helping the cousins to their feet. They looked battered and worse for wear, partially frozen and waterlogged beyond measure, but they were alive. By some grace of nature and the great Goddess, all six captives made it out of the doomed ship to land.

Riana shuddered in relief, but that relief was only momentary. There was still no sign of Horatio.

Duncan and Arin rose on shaking legs, scanning their surroundings.

"Did we make it to the Highlands? I dinna recognize the land," Arin asked in a shivering voice. The poor lad's teeth chattered as he spoke.

Riana shook her head. "Perchance we are on one of the firths. Or we may be on an isle. Either way, we are in better straits than those on that ship."

"And your Roman?" Duncan asked.

Riana's face twitched with fear and worry. She shook her head again.

"I have no' seen him. He is called Horatio."

Turning from the cousins, Riana let her gaze rove across the firth, searching.

"He was no' on a barrel, just swimming. He had more control over his path, I should think. Mayhap he arrived elsewhere?"

"Farther south, then?" Bevan ventured. "The course of the sea pushed the barrels north. Perchance, if we had been able to steer their direction, we may have ended up on the southern edge of the firth, and nay this far in."

"We should head inland," Arin offered. "The man is clever enough. If he does no' see us on the shore wi' him, he may ken that we have gone in search of a smithy and shelter." Arin lifted his hands to let his chains clang.

All eyes riveted on Riana to decide. Her mind was still chilled, and she agonized about making the wrong choice. Is this what 'twas like for her father? Having to make life and death decisions so suddenly? In that moment, Riana had a flash of respect for Ru, who made leadership look like a child's game.

She brought her thoughts back to the shore, now darkening in the gloaming and remnants of the storm. The petrichor settled over the shoreline, still reeling from the havoc wreaked by the rain and lightning. She could smell it, the aftermath of damage and the promise of being washed clean, a revenant of a new day. Riana made her decision.

"Let us take this last light of the day and work our way south to check the shore. 'Tis what Horatio would do for us. If we dinna see him, then we will start inland. A village must be nearby."

"Or Romans," Arin spoke aloud the prospect no one wanted to say.

They had come so far. Riana vowed she'd never allow them to fall into Roman hands again.

The only Roman hands she hoped to see were Horatio's.

⁓

The shoreline rose before them as they stumbled over the stones and around grass clumps, searching for the one Roman who saved them from death.

They held each other upright as they trudged along, their bodies battered and worn and protesting their efforts. They wanted a warm fire, hot food, and soft beds. Traipsing across the firth went against everything their bodies and minds screamed out for.

'Twas almost full dark when a large boulder blocked most of the coastline. The cousins protested crossing it, mumbling that 'twas time to head inland. Iona and Isolde remained silent, and Riana feared for their wits. Had all this chaos driven them mad?

"We shall check this last stretch. If he's no' here, then he's gone in search of a village. Or his fellow soldiers," Bevan directed. His youthful voice carried authority, and the cousins stopped their grumblings.

Riana had braced herself to find nothing. Or worse, to see Horatio's body, lifeless and unmoving. What was left if he threw his caution to the wind to save her, only to die in his efforts? Riana's chest clenched at the image and wiped it from her mind.

She needed to be strong for this small band of people, and such negative thoughts might break her.

Bevan clasped her hand to help Riana climb around the boulder. The tides were going out, another fortunate circumstance, and they easily made their way to the southern point of the firth.

At first, she saw nothing, only lonely rocks and clusters of grass casting the last dark shadows in the rising moonlight. Then one of the dark shapes moved, rolling over with a groan.

Riana burst into a run, dragging poor Bevan behind her. "Horatio!"

***

He was almost to the shore when his body quit. His arms wouldn't move, no matter how much his mind screamed at him that land was there, *right there*, just push. But his arms didn't obey, and Horatio had to believe that he could remain afloat long enough for the waves to beat him to the rocky shoreline. So close.

Closing his eyes was not an option, as he needed to be able to see if he drifted near the shore, lest he knock his head on the rocks that extended into the sea. Oh, the irony of life if he made it across the tumultuous sea, only to break his head open as he reached land.

One final, low wave pushed through, sending him soaring onto the land where he scrambled out of the icy waters. Once he crawled past the tide line, he collapsed, fearing he may never rise again.

Lying on his back, he rested, shivering on a small patch of rocky sand, breathing hard to catch his breath. It was the first moment of a break he'd had since he'd entered that hold, and that moment of rest was crucial. His body had never felt so broken in all his life. Lifting rocks now seemed like a minor chore. He would never complain of it again.

A scuffling sound came from his left, farther up the shoreline, and Horatio turned his head, trying to see if it were Riana and her compatriots or his own Roman soldiers. Several shadowy figures emerged from behind a giant boulder, and he squinted at them, rolling to his side to rise for a better look.

"Horatio!"

His name on Riana's lips was the only healing cure required for his aching body. Suddenly, every pain evaporated as his heart surged in his chest.

They had done it? They both made it to safety?

He hadn't thought such a thing possible. The gods must favor them.

Horatio had one foot planted to rise when Riana's body hit him with enough force to throw him on his back into the sand, where she rained kisses on his face and hair.

His arms encircled her strong body, clutching her close as he caught her mouth, kissing her with all the glory of life that flowed through him. There, on that rocky beach, were only the two of them— they were alive, together, they had survived and found one another's arms. That was the only thing that mattered.

Their tongues danced and touched, exchanging precious breath until a gentle throat clearing to Horatio's right refocused their attention.

"This reunion is tender, but we have greater concerns, aye?" Bevan held his chained hand aloft.

"Oh, yes." Horatio shifted Riana to his side, wild tendrils of her hair wrapping around them. The others who'd been captive in the hold stood with the young Caledonii, their eyes on

Horatio and Riana. "We need to take care of those chains, then get you each on your paths home."

"Do you ken where we are?" Iona's shock had finally begun to wear away, and she spoke for the first time. Frail little Isolde, however, still clung to her sister as she clung to life. Riana feared the wee lass might never be in her right mind again.

"Are we anywhere near where the ship put out to sea?" Riana ventured.

Given their state when they were brought on board, only Horatio had his full senses to take in his surroundings.

But he shook his head in a disheartening movement. "'Twas light when we embarked. And in this dark, I can barely see my own hand before my face, let alone the dock. Did you see anything when you walked on the northern part of the firth?"

"Nay," Riana answered.

"Then we need to make a decision. No matter what, we must move inland to walk with ease. From there, do you want to continue west, or move farther north? How well do you know these lands?"

All eyes focused again on Riana, who chewed her lip. They were cold, wet, and still in chains. She wracked her brain, searching for the best solution, trying to figure out where they were in relation to her village. Avoiding any Romans was most important; finding a Caledonii village was second. And this near to the shore, Romans assuredly covered the land worse than lice on a mangy dog.

"Inland." Her eyes flashed with an authority that would have made her father proud. "Too many Romans litter the seaboard. We will more likely find a village if we move west, away from the shore."

Five pairs of nervous eyes flashed from Riana to Horatio and back. Horatio noted their hesitancy and stood, helping Riana to her feet.

"Your plan is sound. Let us leave the shoreline and find a smith to remove these chains. Perchance he will know a place where we can find a fire and dry bedding for the night."

Chapter Nineteen: A Rag-Tag Band of Travelers

THEIR MOVEMENTS WERE slow over the rocky shoreline, which transformed into gentle hills and thin woods. The night air was brisk, and while it helped dry their clothing, it did little to warm them after their icy swim.

Horatio used the stars to keep them on a set path until they stepped onto a worn trail that led northwest. Hope bloomed in their chests for the first time in days. This path could lead them home.

Soon, a series of fires appeared in the distance, torches lit below the rickety palisade wall surrounding the village. A few lone roundhouses sat in darkness outside the wall, but the port was ajar. Thus far, fate had been on their side. The gods and goddesses smiled again. Riana prayed 'twould stay that way.

They didn't arrive quietly — the clanging of their chains was one sound they were unable to mute. And a grizzled older man exited his doorway, watching them with cautious eyes as they approached.

"Huzzah, good sir!" Horatio greeted the man, whose face scrunched up at being addressed so formally. "We have need of a smith. Have you one in your village?"

"Who are ye to ask for one? Ye appear to be Roman, yet your companions look to be Caledonii, and in poor condition. Who are ye and what are ye doing with those in chains?"

The grizzled man was on guard, naturally, and they had expected it. The sword in his hand, however, was not expected. Horatio, realizing his precarious position with this man, moved to the side to allow Riana and Bevan to step forward.

"Good sirrah. My name is Riana Blogh, daughter of Ru Blogh and close kin to King Gartnaith Blogh. This Roman has helped us escape a dismal fate, and we'd be grateful for your assistance. We are in need of a smith to help us remove these chains. My father, the Caledonii tribe, and the great goddess, will reward ye for any aid ye can provide."

The grizzled man's eyes widened at her short speech. He bowed his head and waved them along the path.

"Come wi' me. Ahearn may still be in his stall."

He led them through the gate and to the left. The blacksmith's forge was darkening, his scorching fires burning low for the night.

"Ahearn! Grab your tools, man, and stoke that flame. These folk have need of ye!"

A banging sound pierced the night, followed by a curse. From the darkness, a mountain of a man emerged, his pink skin and red beard streaked with black and ash. He was bare chested and irritated at being disturbed.

The Maiden of the Storm

"Tort! Ye annoying ass! What brings ye here this late at night to disturb my rest?"

"Ooch, your rest. Ye mean your drink. Get your tools, whatever ye use to break links. The daughter of Ru Blogh needs your help with some chains."

"What —?" the giant said as he regarded the pathetic crowd just outside his forge. "Daughter of Ru? Why is she here, this far from her village?" His shadowy eyes flicked to Horatio. "And why is she with this Roman?"

The grizzled man, Tort, waved him off. "They can share their tale after. For now, get your tools and help the lass!"

Grunting, Ahearn stared at the old man for a span of several heartbeats before resigning himself. He turned into his stall and retrieved something behind him.

What he held up sent a shot of panic down Riana's spine. In one monstrous hand he grasped a tapered level that ended in a sharp edge. The other hand clasped a hammer larger than Riana's head.

She paled when he gestured at her and Bevan.

"Lay your irons here, on the anvil."

Bevan had to drag Riana to the metal table. Her legs weakened and she thought she might swoon, but she masked it with a hard expression. They placed their hands on either side, the heavy iron chain laying across the top. The smith positioned the lever at the joint of two links, and with a shocking smack of the hammer that caused Riana to jump and shriek, the chain between the two of them fell away.

"Now, place your hand here," Ahearn directed.

Riana paused, gathering her courage to put her frail hand under this man's sharp tools, when Bevan thrust his arm out. It sat atop the anvil like a captured animal.

Ahearn nodded at Bevan's bravery, then placed the lever at the rivet joining the cuff latch. One strong tap and the rivet top

The Maiden of the Storm

separated from the shaft, and the shackle sprung apart with a creak. Bevan's hand was free. Ahearn did the same for his other hand, and a look of stark relief passed over Bevan's face as he rubbed his red, ravaged wrists.

Riana thrust her hand to the anvil without hesitation, waiting to be freed. She'd only been in shackles for a few days. How had Horatio lasted months? She closed her eyes and shivered while Ahearn dispatched her irons, and the weight of the chains fell away.

Everyone's release went just as smoothly, except for Isolde who sobbed and protested, certain she'd end up handless. Horatio and Bevan held her still as Ahearn removed her manacles.

The look of relief on the young lassie's face was more than they could bear, and another weight lifted from Riana's shoulders when the girl rubbed her wrists and cried with joy into Iona's *léine*.

"So," Ahearn said as he put his tools back in their place, "how did ye end up here?"

Tort set up bedding in his small house, all seven of them squeezing around the hearth, finally warm and bellies full after a gracious meal, and a rough splint for Horatio's finger, all provided by their host.

Over their supper, they learned they were in Arbroath, near several Roman encampments, including Longforgan, where their fateful ship had set sail. The sisters only had to travel a day or so north to return to their village of Kirriemuir. Tort offered to find his village *Imannae* on the morrow to escort the lassies home.

The cousins, living much farther west near Loch Lomond, would set out with Riana and Horatio. Riana's village of Kilsyth was along their way. With packs of food and a night of rest, Arin assured Tort that they could make the journey home on their own once they passed the Roman camps.

After their plans were set and they settled for the night, Riana found it difficult to fall asleep. Adjusting her covering, she nestled into Horatio, who bed down right behind her.

She rolled over so her face was a breath from his. She said nothing, only locked her eyes on his face.

Horatio's entire face was a patchwork of bruises, cuts, burns and wear. While they had been through so much in this single day, Horatio had worked himself to the bone to make sure they were safe from the hands of the Romans and the death-trap that was the Roman galley.

Her eyes roved over his skin, counting every injury as though each wound was a wound on her own heart. She lifted her hand to his face, tracing the weary lines of his strong features.

"I can no' believe ye found me," Riana whispered against his skin. "I believe in the will of the gods and goddesses, but when ye escaped, I had no faith of ever seeing ye again, no matter what we promised. Is this what fate is?"

Horatio pressed her fingertips to his mouth, kissing each one.

"I don't know much of fate or of the gods. I'm not a learned man. I'm a warrior. And from what I know of the military and war, often we make plans, but better plans, something we never expected lands at our feet. The ether above," Horatio's gaze flicked toward the thatched roof, "has more secrets and plans than any man can know."

He paused and kissed the tip of her nose. "I have to think that something out there — gods, fate, whatever it is, rewarded you. All good deeds echo in eternity, and that fate pulled you back from the netherworld with that echo."

"And the others?" Riana asked.

"They were just fortunate enough to be with you."

Riana's eyes widen into shiny green saucers. "I'd nay call being chained in the hold of a ship fortunate."

"You must look at it another way. If they'd not been with you, had they been on a different ship, or even another part of this ship, then they would have perished, or been sold into slavery, or worse. Instead, they were with you, and rescued and now on their way home."

Horatio kissed the tiny smile that tugged at her cheek. "And look at me," he continued.

"What of ye?"

"I was enslaved, yet I'd not have changed it for the riches of King Croesus. Because of that, I met you, fell in love with you, and was able to save you when it mattered most."

Riana's breath caught.

"Ye love me?"

Horatio's chest vibrated as he gave a tired laugh, his large hand encircling her waist to pull her closer. The heavy weight of his hand on her lower back was more comforting than the fire.

"How can you not know?" His eyes crinkled in humor. "It's not just any woman I risk my life to rescue, after all."

His earnest face tore at her heart. Horatio wore his emotions so plainly — no guile or introspection. Riana too often had to wear a stoic mask, and sharing emotions so freely was strange to her. She rested her palm against his face – the face she'd come to adore so deeply, the face she'd been willing to risk punishment or death to save.

"Since I also risked my own skin to help ye escape, I guess that means I love ye as well."

She twined her fingers in his rich hair, enjoying the silky feel of his sea-worn locks against her fingertips. "What does this mean for us now?"

"Well, the Roman army will think us dead, drowned in the sea. That releases me from my military obligations. I was thinking 'twould be best if I escort you back to your village so your family knows you are unhurt."

"I can no' stay there, no' with ye. I can no' have ye live in the same village where ye were enslaved."

"Then after we greet your family, we can pack up any of your belongings, and we will strike out, find our own way. But perchance —" Horatio stopped himself short.

"Perchance what?"

"Perchance we might reside in your village long enough to celebrate our wedding?"

Riana's worried face alighted with joy. "Are ye sure ye want to stay in the Highlands? With the Caledonii? After everything that has happened?"

Horatio brushed her hair from her forehead and kissed her there.

"Wherever you are, I want to stay with you."

Morning came too soon. Though Tort vowed he'd safeguard the sisters' journey into protective hands, Bevan stepped forward to stand next to Iona.

"Ye dinna have to fret for the lasses, Daughter of Ru. I will escort them as well. They will no' be alone."

The Maiden of the Storm

Riana clasped Bevan's hand. "Are ye certain of this, Bevan? Ye are missed at home."

"Aye." Bevan nodded. "Yet, I am not needed there. I am needed here. Tell my family I am well and will return home in due time."

Riana tipped her head at the young *Imannae*, respecting his aim to live up to the reputation of his title. No longer in training, the past days of tribulation had forged him into a true Caledonii warrior.

After tearful hugs to Riana, Bevan and the sisters headed north with several of Tort's kin.

The grizzled Tort and the mountain-sized Ahearn gave each of them a small packet of food and tools to help them on their journey home.

"I have naught to give ye in return," Riana told the older man when he hugged her goodbye.

"My children are gone to the far winds. I live on my own, but with the grace of my tribe and villagers like Ahearn, I have more than I need. To thank me, if ye have the chance in the future to do a good turn, then that will suffice."

"Then she has more than paid that in return," Horatio told him, clapping the man on the back.

The cousins bid the men farewell, and they set off into the bright light of morning.

The lands sparkled in the daylight, washed clean from the torrential rains. Now, in the sun's clear rays, every drop of dew sparkled on the refreshed landscape. 'Twas as though the goddess Brigid herself had cleansed the land – their prize for weathering the mighty storm.

Duncan and Arin parted ways with Riana and Horatio just south of Kilsyth early the following day. Wishing the cousins safe travels, Riana and Horatio continued toward Riana's village.

The wooden palisade appeared in the horizon; a more welcoming sight Riana could not imagine. Her heart quickened, fluttering against her breast in anticipation and nervousness. She'd not left the village under the best terms, and she didn't know who yet lived or perished under the Roman attack that led to her entrapment. What might she encounter on the other side of the gates?

Horatio must have sensed her trepidation, and he tugged on her hand, so she turned to face him.

"Are you nervous?"

"Aye," Riana answered, keeping her eyes focused on the horizon. "I dinna ken what welcome I will receive."

"'Tis fair," Horatio agreed. "But you can rest in knowing that no matter the welcome that comes from the other side of the port gate, you will have me ever by your side."

With a strong finger, he tipped her chin up so her face was close to his, and he sealed that promise with a kiss.

Chapter Twenty: A Fine Welcome Home

NIALL STOOD AT the gate, his eyes deceiving him.

Though he and Dunbraith had been left for dead on the side of the path near the wall surrounding the Roman camp, they had picked themselves up and helped each other stumble back to the village. Several *Imannae* found them shortly after they started for Kilsyth, and they returned to Kilsyth a broken mess.

Still bruised and bandaged, courtesy of Aila, Niall was recovering, as he was hale and in robust health to begin with. He'd begun resuming his post at the gate the day after he made it home, as though he needed to prove himself after the attack.

Now, he wondered if he was mayhap more injured than Aila claimed, for the vision before him must be his imagination. It had to be false.

He rubbed at his eyes and peered again, and this time the figures were closer, marching up the trail toward the village in the brilliant light of day.

"Eian! Cuinn! Send for Ru!" he yelled over his shoulder. "And Aila!" he added as an afterthought. The gods only knew what injuries they may have.

Riana, daughter of Ru and she of the wild, wine-hued hair, fierce green eyes, and firm back, sauntered toward him with, was that the *Roman*?

Niall thought he *must* have a serious head injury that was affecting his brain. Riana was gone, abducted by the Romans, and the Roman had escaped to his people. While it was possible that Riana may have found her way home, why did the Roman come as well? Why did he return to the same place that had enslaved him?

Cuinn returned, his black hair making his bright green eyes seem brighter. And they flashed with curiosity. His chest hitched, and he panted heavily from running to and fro in his task.

"What is it, Niall? Why did we rush to retrieve Ru?"

Niall said nothing, only tipped his head toward the road. Cuinn's verdant eyes widened with disbelief.

"Nay. 'Tis nay Riana?" Then he squinted at the couple approaching. "And who's with her?"

"The Roman," Niall answered in a flat voice.

The past fortnight had bordered on madness. Now he was convinced 'twas a dream, or an injury. Or sheer madness? Events like this didn't happen in this oft unforgiving world.

Yet here she was, running toward Niall who opened his arms as Riana threw herself into them.

"Oh, Niall! Ye are alive! What a sight ye are!"

Niall gaped at Riana. The reality of her in his arms, the impossible was made real. He stuttered as he tried to make sense of her presence.

"Riana! How —? Are —?" He didn't know what question to ask first, then his eyes flicked to the Roman. "What are ye doing here, Roman?"

"Horatio," Riana interjected, disentangling herself from Niall. "His name is Horatio, and he is the only reason I am standing before ye today."

She spoke with an air of authority, one Niall well recognized and which sounded so much like her father. Cuinn reached forward to embrace his chieftain's daughter, and Niall turned toward the Roman.

"Ooch, Roman. Horatio. Ye are the man who brought Riana back to us?"

Reserved and wary, Horatio nodded briefly. Niall extended his arm to him.

"Then I have to thank ye and welcome ye into our village."

Horatio stared at the arm for several breaths, surprised at the offer from the man who had been his prison guard. He flicked his deep-set gaze to Riana, then reached out his own arm and clasped Niall's forearm in his hand.

"I appreciate your welcome."

"Riana! Ri!" the chieftain's deep voice bellowed across the yard to the port gate, and Riana lifted her head to the sound. An exuberant smile split her face.

"Father!"

She broke from Cuinn and ran as fast as her weary legs could carry her. Her ragged skirts whipped around her ankles, trying to slow her. But nothing slackened her pace until she was in her father's arms again.

"Riana, we thought we'd lost ye," Ru's rich, familiar voice cracked as he pressed his face into his daughter's hair. "Had anything happened to ye, 'twould have been my fault. I let my anger control my decisions. Can ye forgive me?"

Riana nuzzled in the comfort of her father's tunic as he sobbed. He seemed thinner, less powerful, and she wondered what her brief absence had done to him.

"'Tis naught to forgive. Ye did no' ken that the Romans were on the prowl. We can lay the blame at their feet alone."

Her father stiffened in her arms.

"Then what is he doing here?" That recognizable Ru fury rose in his voice. Riana tightened her grip on her father.

"Nay, Father. 'Tis no' what ye think. I'd nay be standing here before ye today if no' for Horatio."

Ru glared at the bronzed man who stayed near the gate, surrounded by Caledonii. Horatio stood tall and proud, not shirking under the harsh, accusatory glare.

"What do ye mean? He is an escaped slave, a Roman, and all blame resides with him."

"Nay. He was being sent away by his army. We ended up on the same ship, and only by the will of the goddess did he learn where I was held. When the storm rose, it battered the ship. Horatio took advantage of the chaos to help us escape."

Ru's eyes shifted about. "Us?"

Riana's gaze softened at her dear father. She reached a hand to Horatio, beckoning him to join her side. The pinched look of confusion on Ru's red face only tightened.

"I shall tell you everything, Father." Riana peered around Ru and smiled at her eager sisters and Tege standing behind him. "Let us go home. I have a tale to spin for ye."

Ru gave Horatio a wizened glare before following his family to their roundhouse.

"I am pleased ye are home safe, lassie," Ru told Riana in a sad voice as her sisters cleared the remains of their meal. "I'll admit, I had no' expected to see ye again."

Riana leaned against her father's broad shoulder, understanding how difficult 'twas for him to say those words. Like Riana, Ru was not a man to share deep emotion.

And the last time they were in the same room, she'd seen only anger in his eyes. Terms of endearment were a welcome change.

"I, too, am glad to have made it back. The Caledonii lands are my home. I dinna ken how I would have survived anywhere else."

"Ye are too much like your father," Ru said with a wisp of tenderness. "Ye are dedicated to the land, to your tribe. Mayhap I should have raised ye as more of a lassie and less of a second in command."

His lamentations struck home. He'd often treated Riana more as the son he never had, and while it showed in her oft brash behavior, it also strengthened her and made her more capable than she thought possible.

"Nay, Father. Never regret that. I am only here because of that strength, of the way ye raised me. Weel, that and him."

Riana flicked her head at her Roman. He sat by the fire, his bronzed skin reflecting the light of the flames as Aila worked him over with her poultices and flax strips. She'd done her best to treat that wrongly bent finger and was now applying a salve to his face.

Her father's pale green eyes, the mirror of Riana's, assessed the stranger who presently sat as a guest in the chieftain's home. His thick ruddy beard didn't hide the twitch of ire that caught his lips.

"I dinna care for the lad," Ru admitted, "But he saved ye and returned ye to us, so he will always have my respect and thanks for that."

Riana cut her eyes to Ru and inhaled deeply.

"Ooch, if ye dinna care for the man in your home, ye shall really detest what I am about to tell ye."

Ru stiffened. "I dinna think I want to hear it."

A knowing smile pulled at Riana's lips. She shifted her face back to Horatio and graced him with a tender look. Ru watched the movement and groaned from the depths of his chest.

"Oh, dinna tell me."

Riana outright giggled at her father's discomfort.

"Aye, Father, and the news is bad, then worse. We shall be wed as soon as we can. He will ask ye for my hand either tonight or tomorrow, and we will marry right after. Send for the *druidai*." She paused, taking her father's calloused hand in her own before continuing. "And then we must depart. 'Tis nay proper for us to live here, aye? But we will settle in a nearby village, as I dinna want to live too far from my close kin."

"What if I say nay?" Ru tried to sound like the authoritative father but failed.

Riana shrugged. "Then we will leave on the morrow, and ye will rob my sisters of seeing me wed."

"Oh, my Ri, the thought pains my heart. Ye are formidable, to be sure."

"I learned it from my father," she told him, returning her gaze to the hearth.

Chapter Twenty-One: What Happens When Love Wins

A GLOWERING RU stood to the side as Tege and Riana's sisters stood under the mighty oak, coronets of thistle and bog myrtle adorning their hair.

The *druidai,* Fionn, waited next to Ru under the tree's canopy. Though the Romans tried to eradicate the druids, they had been unsuccessful. A few yet remained in the Caledonii Highlands, and Fionn dressed the part. His long, pale *breacan* brushed his bare feet and was tied at the waist with a leather girdle. Bright feathers were woven into his unruly locks. His dress, together with the serious expression on his face, indicated the reverence by which he held this ceremony.

Tege and Ru's daughters had used flowers and branches to create a wide circle under the tree; then Horatio walked out from the nearby brush. Riana's sisters rushed him, cheering and fawning as they pushed him toward the circle.

Horatio felt refined in his borrowed tunic that clung loosely about his chest and shoulders. The leather belt, borrowed from Ru, was as tight as he could make it, and it still hung on his hips, the creamy flaxen tunic draping almost to his knees. He was barelegged, following Celtic fashion, and barefoot, to connect to the earth, as Aila had explained to him.

Riana sashayed to the circle, just behind Horatio and surrounded by the members of her village. Small children jumped and giggled next to her, twirling brightly colored ribbons in the air. Riana's wild tresses were pulled back under a circlet of heather and thistle, the purples and whites bright against her fiery hair. Her milky skin glowed under thin blue woad lines on her cheeks and the glinting torc at her neck, while her fierce eyes gazed straight ahead at the lean man who had changed every fiber of her world.

Her gown, a creamy color similar to Horatio's and edged in deep green and blue threads, had wide sleeves that swallowed her slender arms. She too abandoned her foot coverings, keeping her skin directly on the earth.

Horatio stood just outside the floral ring, and once Riana reached him, they entered the ring together. The *druidai* began chanting the *Caim* wedding protection prayer:

> *"Bless to me the sky that is above me,*
> *Bless to me the ground that is beneath me,*
> *Bless to me the friends — furry, feathered, or fronded —*
> *who are around me,*
> *Bless to me the love of the Three Deep within me and*
> *encircling me*
> *and the greater community of life."*

He then withdrew an oblong stone from under his cape. He took Horatio's hand, rested it on the stone, sang another chant, then lay Riana's hand atop the stone, her fingers overlapping Horatio's.

The *druidai* removed the stone and placed it in the crook of the tree, then waved his arms at the children in the crowd. They came forward, handing over the brilliant ribbons, which Fionn wound around Horatio and Riana's hands, binding them as his chanting became more powerful, more commanding.

After they repeated the *druidai's* words of devotion to each other, he took a small knife from his girdle. Before Horatio could react, the man cut his palm with a flourish.

Horatio winced and wanted to jerk his hand away, but the *druidai* held him tight and flicked the dirk again, slicing at Riana. She didn't move, having expected the stab. Fionn pressed their wounds together and had Horatio recite his vow to Riana. Then 'twas Riana's turn, and she made her claim on Horatio in a loud voice.

To Horatio, the entire ceremony passed in a heartbeat, and before he knew it, Riana was kissing him. Their lips joined in a celebration, not only of their union, but of their life they managed to save. All those gathered to witness the wedding cheered.

Except Ru. His heavy arms remained crossed over his expansive chest, and his glower never left the couple.

Platters of food sat on a low table near the center village. Children snuck sweetbreads and fruity *cranachan* into their mouths as they ran among the adults. Lovers stole kisses in the shadows of the village, heather ale and mead exchanged freely between their wanton lips.

Riana's sisters ogled the *Imannae* and other young men of the tribe while at the same time hugging and fawning over Riana.

Horatio, however, didn't have the chance to celebrate, having been cornered by the glowering chieftain.

"Ye ken that I sacrificed a potential powerful match for Riana to permit her to wed ye."

Horatio had no voice. What did one say to that? He lowered his head in silence.

"Instead, I let her wed ye. I didn't want to lose her again. I canna lose my daughter, do ye ken my words?"

The ferocity emanating from Ru was lost when Horatio lifted his gaze to the man's face. Ru's eyes softened as he gazed upon his eldest child.

"When ye go to your new village, make sure 'tis nay far from here. I expect to see her regularly."

"Yes, we will settle close by." That was a promise he could easily make. He'd already made it to Riana, and for her, he would promise the world.

"I thank ye again for saving my daughter. I treated her shabbily after your, uh, disappearance. I want to make it up to her, if I can."

Riana came up to them, smiling at her father. They embraced, Riana getting lost in the gigantic arms of her father, and Horatio grinned at the chieftain.

"I don't think that will be a worry," Horatio told him in a low voice.

Riana and Horatio shared a tented space off the side of her father's roundhouse. Tege had offered them a pallet inside, near the hearth, but the newly wedded couple craved far more privacy than the roundhouse could provide, especially under the watch of her father and her nosy sisters.

The rough fabric pulled taught from the roundhouse to the ground, atop another layer of thick burlap that shielded them from the cool grass. Several layers of plaid served as their bed and coverings, and 'twas all they needed for the night.

Shedding their clothing in desperate haste under the blankets, Horatio tried to take his time with his new bride, kissing her pale skin with reverence, as though being with her, being her husband, was a marvel from the gods. And as his mouth worked its way over her breasts and down her belly, he told her as much.

"Ye are a gift I never expected, more valuable than any gold or jewels."

Riana sighed at the sensation of his lips on her woman's mound and the weight of his words in her ears. She moaned when his lips parted her intimate folds.

"And this, this is the nectar of the gods, granted to me this night and for all nights. And I promise to drink from it often."

Then his tongue was touching her most delicate skin, light at first, then the flat of his tongue dragging over the bud that was the center of her pleasure.

Riana writhed and moaned under the work of his tongue, begging for release. Only when Horatio felt he had played her enough, that she was at her height, did he wrap his lips around the bud and suck.

Her insides exploded like lightening hitting a tree, every part of her splintering, and she shrieked his name. Her legs clenched, holding his head in place as she rose higher and higher, calling out to Horatio and the goddess when she reached her full moment.

Then Horatio slid atop her, kissing her lips so she tasted the salty nectar of herself, and he thrust his quivering staff into her welcome sheath. He fit without flaw, a perfect meeting of heat and earth.

She rode his thrusts, matching his movements, letting her excitement build again as Horatio's breathing grew more ragged. He chanted her name in her ear, a prayer to the gods, and his voice grew in urgency to match his tremulous motions. Then he clenched above her, calling out her name once more as his seed poured into her in a rush.

Horatio held himself over her for several harsh breaths before lowering his head to rest on Riana's own panting breasts.

They lay in the still darkness, relishing the fullness of life as they collected themselves.

Horatio's dark hair contrasted against her moonlight skin, and she twined her fingers in his recent growth. 'Twas obvious he hadn't cut it when he returned to his contingent.

"I am surprised to be here," he said in a voice muffled by her breast.

"What, that I should wed ye? Or that we are here, back in my village?"

Horatio lifted his head, the sparkle of his eyes barely visible in the dark.

"No, here. Alive. When I left you, I vowed to return to you in some way, no matter what. Then, when I saw you on the ship, chained, 'twas as if someone put a knife in my heart. Your captivity, your pain, was killing me. And I'd have slain every man aboard that ship to free you. When the storm rose and the ship shattered, I made a silent promise that, regardless of what happened to me, I would make sure you survived."

He nuzzled her soft breasts, as if in assurance that she was truly here, lying under him, and that she was not a dream.

"But ye survived," she whispered.

"Yes, here I am with you, instead of in Elysium, the land of the dead. While Elysium is the promise of every filled desire, I don't want it. Because you are here, and you are the fulfillment of every longing I have. I had not known that Elysium could be here in my arms."

Riana lay her palm on his cheek, the sharp bones of his face pressing against her hand, assuring her that he was here, he was real, and he wasn't a dream.

"Everything I have ever wanted is in my arms," she said to him, her own emotions taking hold. "And if ye are a dream, then I never want to wake. I want ye here with me always."

He kissed her, moving his lips from her forehead to her cheeks before finding her eager mouth.

"You have me. I am yours to command. Always."

The End

Excerpt from The Maiden of the Grove

The next book in the Celtic Highland Maidens series – coming soon!

Aila rushed to Fion's side within moments of his brother arriving at her father's roundhouse. His askew hair and panicked eyes told Aila more than his words begging her to come right away. Maeve helped Aila gather her herbals into a worn leather satchel.

"What do ye think, Aila?" she asked in hushed tones.

Tege, their stepmother was asleep behind her curtain and their father had not yet returned from the village of Twechar. Life in their village of Kilsyth had been quiet, uneventful, in their father's absence, which made them all feel relieved. Nothing was worse than dramatic events unfolding whilst the chieftain was away.

Aila shrugged. Fion was the second to fall ill with this harsh sickness that settled into the chest. The victim coughed and coughed until they lost the energy to cough anymore. Her first patient had recovered after days of ferocious care by Aila. Fion, though, was not as hale. He'd been a sickly sort since birth, and Aila feared for his recovery.

"I can only hope that my herbals, skills, and the power of the goddess Airmid will heal him. I worry that the limit of my abilities will be exceeded with him."

Maeve gave Aila a tight smile as she pulled the strings of the satchel together. Aila grabbed the satchel and threw her *arasaid* over her shoulders and ran out the door.

The air was cool as autumn cast its multi-chromatic cloak across the Highlands. The grass under her bare feet was crisp, starting to give up its green life to sleep for the winter. Brilliant reds and yellows tinged the trees surrounding the village, but they went unnoticed by Aila who was singularly focused on her trek to Fion's roundhouse.

She chanted to herself as she ran, a mix of a prayer to Airmid and a list of what she must do to help Fion recover. When she reached his home, she entered without waiting for permission.

The sounds of Fion choking and gasping filled the roundhouse, and the family was clustered around a body lying near the hearth. The air inside the house was warm, too warm, and not just from illness. Panic, fear, exertion, were all taking their toll, and from the noises Fion emitted, she needed to work quickly.

"Move, back away. Let the man breathe," Aila commanded. She was not known for her social graces or tactful tones. Curt and to the point best described the chieftain's second eldest daughter.

The family instantly obeyed, except for Fion's mother who cradled his head on her lap. Her pleading eyes caught Aila's focused gaze.

"He was fine, Aila, fine, until this afternoon. I mean, he'd been coughing o'course, but no' badly. No' like this . . ." Her words faded into a prayerful plea.

'Twas an expression with which Aila was familiar. Her patients and their families begged for relief, for the life of their loved one, and often saw Aila like the Goddess Airmid in human form. And as much as Aila tried to disabuse them of that notion, it never worked. They begged, pleaded, and bartered for the lives of their loved ones. Mothers, as Aila well knew, were the most ardent.

Aila prided herself on her skills while lamenting her lack of training. The healer crone who had begun training Aila died several years ago, leaving Aila as the only healer in her village.

Though Aila did her best to learn everything she could about the healing arts, and was even considered one of the greatest healers in all the tribe, she chastised herself over her limitations.

In fact, earlier in the year, one of the men had not been paying attention to his axe and clipped off several toes through his leather boots. His kin raced for Aila, and she treated his missing toes, covering the gaping wound in a mix of fern and bog myrtle after 'twas cauterized. But the bones . . . she'd been horrified to see so much of the foot exposed and damaged — 'twas not something her wisewoman had taught her to treat. Doing the best she could with her materials, she covered the foot and bandaged it, and even fashioned a type of crutch and binding to prevent the man from walking on it directly while it healed.

She'd been lauded over her quick thinking and skills, yet the man's foot bones didn't heal as Aila had hoped, and he now walked with a limp. Kinny was happy just to be walking at all, but Aila saw this as a failure. From the gossip in the village, so did some of her tribe.

That failure weighed on her like a yoke. What had she missed? What could she have done differently? Why didn't the bones heal as she thought they should? Those questions plagued her — her mentor, the crone, had not finished her training. What value did a partial healer have in the village? Or the tribe at large? The Caledonii were a warrior people. What happened when their healer was unable to keep them in that stature?

This cough. 'Twas thicker, and poor Fion choked as he coughed, unable to rest. That was a basic tenant of her training. A body unable to rest was a body unable to heal. She pursed her lips as she listened to Fion's chest. The rattling was unmistakable.

Nessa entered on silent feet, joining Aila to assist. The young woman had been working with Aila for the past year, herself training as a healer for her own village. Thus far, she'd been a staunch assistant, easing Aila's burden. She handed Aila her own bag of herbals and a brown *quaich* bowl and pestle.

A mix of pine oil and goose grease might help him breathe easier and allow him to sleep. But the cough was well entrenched. Rest would only do so much unless she managed to treat the cough itself.

Make him cough more? Have him expel whatever was in his chest? Or have him rest for the night and see what a night of sleep might do for him? The worst part of being a healer was that decisive moment meant life or death for those under her hands. The purplish half-moons under Fion's eyes, however, made that decision for her.

If you love this book, be sure to leave a review! Reviews are life blood for authors, and I appreciate every review I receive!

Love what you read? Want more from Michelle? Sign up for her email and more at her website:

https://mddalrympleauthor.wixsite.com/home

A Note on History

This time period in history has always fascinated me – from the stories of Boudicca to the druids to the gods and goddesses. And of course, the ancient Highland background. One of my favorite romances focused on the story of a Roman soldier and the Celtic woman he wanted to be with. It was a great book, even if I did read it thirty years ago and forgot the title.

A few notes – the Celts were only called that by the Romans, as several groups were called celts throughout Europe. The Insular Celts were specific to the British Isles and predate the Picts. In fact, they are considered the early ancestors to the later Picts, thusly called because of their painted faces and bodies. During the time period of this book, the tribes were separate entities, even by villages, and only into the 5th century did they start to become a more unified Pictish group, according to historians.

Not much is known about the ancient Celts. We have some of their writing on ancient stones, and some remnants and artifacts – including their conical wheelhouses. Even the ancient Romans wrote a bit about them, but other than that, not much is known.

I also hope I've done justice to the amazing religious beliefs of the ancient Insular Celts. I have read about their myths, festivals, and belief systems, but I do not actively practice them myself. We also don't know exactly how these people would have celebrated or practiced the belief system variation that is present today – so some creative inventions were necessary to present the ideology, keep the feel of the time period, and fit the narrative of the story. I hope I've painted the Celtic beliefs and practices in the best light possible.

For the entire series, I've researched and done my best to reflect the culture and people of the time, of course taking creative licensing when necessary to fit the story.

A thank you to my readers –

I would like to extend a heartfelt thank you for taking a chance and reading this first book in my new series! I only hope it captured your hearts and attention as much as it did mine.

I would not have been able to write this if it weren't for you, my loyal readers, who keep buying my books and encouraging me to write. You have my eternal gratitude. I will endeavor to keep producing the best stories I can for you.

A huge thank you to the myriad of websites and online sources that provided so much needed information. In particular, I need to thank the admins of two websites: owlsdaugher.com and waymarkers.net for the festival and wedding incantations presented in the book.

As always, I also need to thank my kids and family for always supporting me. Even though writing takes me away from them, they are my best cheerleaders. Maybe they like it -- mommy isn't bugging them if she's writing!

I also need to thank my Facebook groups and writing colleagues who provide guidance and advice when needed. We are a tight-knit group, and you all are so wonderful for helping me along this path.

Finally, I would be remiss if I didn't thank my hubby, Michael, the man in my life who has been so supportive of my career shift to focus more on writing, and who makes a great sounding board for ideas. Thank you, babe, for putting up with this and for being my own Happily Ever After.

If you liked *The Maiden of the Storm*, please leave me a review!

About the Author

Michelle Deerwester-Dalrymple is a professor of writing and an author. She started reading when she was 3 years old, writing when she was 4, and published her first poem at age 16. She has written articles and essays on a variety of topics, including several texts on writing for middle and high school students. She has written fifteen books under a variety of pen names and is also slowly working on a novel inspired by actual events. She lives in California with her family of seven.

Find Michelle on your favorite social media sites and sign up for her newsletter here:

https://linktr.ee/mddalrympleauthor

Also by the Author:

<u>Glen Highland Romance</u>
To Dance in the Glen – Book 1
The Lady of the Glen – Book 2
The Exile of the Glen – Book 3
The Jewel of the Glen – Book 4
The Seduction of the Glen – Book 5
The Warrior of the Glen – Book 6 coming soon!
An Echo in the Glen – Book 7 coming soon!

<u>The Celtic Highland Maidens</u>
The Maiden of the Storm
The Maiden of the Grove – coming soon

<u>As M. D. Dalrymple: Men in Uniform Series</u>
Night Shift – Book 1
Day Shift – Book 2
Overtime – Book 3
Holiday Pay – Book 4
School Resource Officer -- Book 5
Holdover – Book 6 coming soon

Printed in Great Britain
by Amazon